Almost every adult in the neighborhood had a Title. It was either Don or Doña, Tío or Tía, Suegra or Fulano de Tal. Never understood the last one, but I hear Fulano is well known. At least the older people had titles ...

... So we know who to respect. If they have a title, then they are well respected. At least here on Wyckoff Street.

... Even though our neighborhood was considered by many to be a dangerous place, none of us felt that way. I guess that's because we knew everyone, and everyone knew us. And we all looked out for each other.

... Mami would know exactly where we were and what we did, each and every day. And she was very happy to let us know this.

"What were you doing on Fulton Street today?" she questioned. "Didn't I tell you no further than Court Street?"

... "But Mami, how did you know?", I asked.

With a smirk she replied, "I have my spies."

I always wondered who her spies were. Was it Don Julio, who always brought us Spanish bread? Or was it Doña Idalia, who made the best pasteles around? Or was it Doña Rivera, who sold Limber de Leche, a frozen treat, from in front of her house? Maybe it was Don Paco, who sold snow cones, which we called Piraguas, in the summer and who was always yelling at his son Papo.

Whomever it was, Mami had good spies; probably better than the FBI or the CIA.

Cover Art: A cityscape (background) from the perspective of a Piraguas (Snow cone) cart (foreground). The Piraguas Cart has the umbrella and the bottles of syrup, which are used to flavor the Piraguas.

Cover Art by: Wook Jin Jung

TACO
John E. DeJesus

WHAT READERS ARE SAYING ...

The book was excellent. I could not put it down. I read it several times.

Nancy S.

The book was great. TACO made me laugh and smile.

Idalia O.

TACO was hard to put down. Even more enjoyable the second time.

David D.

A yummy, yummy read. Made me wish there were more.

Nady O.

It's a fun book to read. TACO brought me back to my childhood days. I definitely recommend it. Very enjoyable.

Hazel M.

A jewel. Attracted by the cover, enticed by the blurb, captivated by the story. TACO is a wondrous delight. I recommend it to all.

JP K.

TACO
John E. DeJesus

WHAT READERS ARE SAYING …

I grew up in Brooklyn and live in Chicago. I miss those old Brooklyn days. I started reading and finished it. My mom was Doña Paloma and my mom had spies that looked out for us. Brought back good memories.

Roland R.

I enjoyed the misadventures of TACO.

Eddie L.

Exciting reading which brought me back in time to my youth in Brooklyn.

Eddie C.

Absolutely enjoyed the book. It was heart warming and nostalgic.

Maggie P.

I really liked the book. I started reading it because my mother was and I saw it put smiles on her face. I found it to be very emotional.

Elena P.

TACO
John E. DeJesus

TACO
John E. DeJesus

WHAT READERS ARE SAYING ...

The author, John DeJesus, captures the essence of a young boy who wants to bring joy to his neighborhood by selling snow cones; even though his life is plagued with sadness and heartbreak.

Romeo L.

I found myself flipping through page after page of your book. Strangely familiar, it brought back many of my own childhood memories of growing up. The unique chapter structure made it light and easy to read. Touching and funny it was a thoroughly enjoyable book that I would recommend to anyone young or young at heart.

Olivier S

If you grew up in El Barrio when you were a kid, this book will touch you. I was able to relate to Taco's stories. The book made me laugh but it was also sad. I could not put the book down. Hazzah! for Taco and all the people who have experienced one or many of his stories while they were kids too. This book is the one that will never sit in someone's closet. Must share with friends. ;)

Maritza V.

TACO tugs at your heartstrings.

Reynaldo C.

TACO
John E. DeJesus

WHAT READERS ARE SAYING ...

I GIVE IT FIVE STARS!! I highly recommend this book. I read it and it brought me back to my childhood days when I was growing up. It has a combination of everything! Once I started reading it, I could not put the book down. This book is great for everyone of all ages! A+

CC L.

I just finished Taco. I have to say I didn't see that coming. You made me cry. I loved it! Thought it was so creative to write it from a kids point of view; how they view situations. So different from when you grow up. A slice of a child's life growing up on Wyckoff Street.
I sooo enjoyed it!

Rose G.

When I sat down to read Taco, I had no idea that I would not put it down until I was done. The book is a series of stories about a young Puerto Rico boy growing up in Brooklyn. The story is set in the 1970's and is told with an endearing innocence. Taco took me on an emotional roller-coaster ride. One minute I was laughing. The next, I was angry or sad. I enjoyed that it was a quick read, but not quickly forgotten. Kudos to John E DeJesus, for telling such a compelling story, beautifully.

May Torres- Author of "The Enchanted Island"

TACO
John E. DeJesus

WHAT READERS ARE SAYING ...

John DeJesus' writing evokes the vibrant and zesty streets of his childhood. From the matriarchs of the family who were "Queens" to the bustling aroma of Bustelo coffee and games of stickball. His writing transports and celebrates the importance of family; share it with yours."

Steven Arvanites, Screenwriter, Director, Producer

Easy reading and hard to put down. The author has a way of not only putting you in the physical neighborhood and city but also emotionally - you become part of his family, all those respected, you find yourself respecting them and knowing why. You can feel Taco's conflicts and the pride when wisdom is spoken to him of his conflicts. I'd like to see some more "Taco" short stories with all his experiences and with those characters in this book."

Patti W.

Hola. He terminado de leer su libro Taco. Es un libro fabuloso, espectacular. La manera en que describe usted las experiencias de Taco y de su familia es tan real que me hizo viajar en mi imaginación y regresar a aquellos años de mi niñez en mi Puerto Rico. ¡Lo terminé en mi tiempo libre en casa y en mi trabajo en dos días y me quede con deseos de leer mas! Lo voy a pasar a mis hijas para que lo lean pues les va a encantar.

Elizabeth S.

TACO

John E. DeJesus

TACO
John E. DeJesus

(Reader's Favorite FIVE STARS * * * * *) Taco is a young adult coming of age novel written by John E. DeJesus. Taco and his family moved to Brooklyn, New York, just before he began first grade. His real name was Juan Ortega, but Percy, a class clown, promptly named him Taco, and the name stuck. They lived in a brownstone on Wyckoff Street, with lots of other Puerto Rican families. The elders had titles; they were called Don or Dona, Tio or Tia, and while Taco thought of them as being royalty, Mami explained that the titles were used out of respect. The Dons and Donas seemed to be founts of wisdom and were always dressed as if for a special occasion. Taco's abuela was known as Dona Maria. She insisted that Taco, his brother, Jose, and sister, Inez, call her Dona instead of abuela. She was slim and vivacious, and she loved to dance. Being called a grandmother made her uncomfortable, and indeed she didn't seem to act like an abuela. One day, she had Taco take pictures as she climbed a tree and perched out on a tree limb.

John E. DeJesus's young adult coming of age novel, Taco, is one of those very rare novels that I just didn't want to end. I loved hearing Taco's stories about his life, his mom and siblings, and the world that was Wyckoff Street while he was growing up. I was especially moved by the passages about Don Paco and his son, Papo, who was Taco's unofficial guardian, mentor and friend. The war-time setting of this novel lends a particularly poignant tone as we see the suffering of Papo who returned from the war with one leg

WHAT READERS ARE SAYING ...

(cont) ...missing and tormented by nightmares that would make him cry out in horror in his sleep. DeJesus beautifully paints the image of that city block as a cohesive and self-supporting village, such as was found back in that tropical homeland which still lived in the heart of each and every resident. Watching as the family and Papo ride the Puerto Rican Parade Float is one of the most moving passages I've read in some time. DeJesus includes a glossary of terms used in the book as well as an Author Q&A which is marvelous reading. In it, he discusses reader interest in a follow-up to Taco, and I'm hoping he does decide to write one. This is one unforgettable coming of age tale and a sequel would be a treat indeed. Taco is most highly recommended.

Jack M.

(Reader's Favorite FOUR STARS * * * *) Taco is a light hearted read based on the childhood experiences of Juan Ortega. Juan, affectionately known as Taco, talks about his years growing up in Wyckoff Street in Brooklyn, New York. He resides with his mother, his sister and brother. His mother is Puerto Rican by birth and the entire family is proud of their heritage. Taco's neighborhood is filled with community spirited personalities as many of its members look out for Taco and his siblings and vice versa. Even Taco mentioned that his "familia" not only consisted of his immediate family members, but also those caring members of Wyckoff Street. Taco gave an account of warm memories of occurrences in his community.

WHAT READERS ARE SAYING ...

(cont) ...For example, he mentioned when his grandmother, Dona Maria, used to climb the tree in the park and have her picture taken. He also shared his true desire to sell Snow Cones like Don Paco. Overall, Taco appreciated his neighborhood and loved sharing his memorable experiences.

Taco is an interesting book. It is composed of short chapters which encourages the reader to continue following the storyline with relish. The language used is simple and easy to understand. I love the fact that author John DeJesus provided a detailed account of the main character's childhood. These descriptive escapades make you pause and reflect on your own childhood days. You might ask yourself were yours as memorable and fun filled as Taco's? This in turn displays the writer's skill in making readers identify with Taco. Despite the revelation that Taco lost some pertinent persons in his life, like his grandmother, he still had an innocence about him as well as a positive outlook on life. I loved the fact that the author mixed the good with the bad as this reflects the realities of life. Taco is a lovely book and I recommend it to all readers.

Valerie R.

WHAT READERS ARE SAYING ...

(Reader's Favorite FOUR STARS * * * *) Taco by John E. DeJesus is a collection of micro-stories written by Taco, a young Puerto Rican boy living in Brooklyn with his mother and two younger siblings, José and (Inez). The collection of stories spans a few years, from the end of the '60s to the beginning of the '70s.

The tales are full of reminiscences and nostalgia, detailing in a very personal way what is was like growing up in a Puerto Rican community in the US in those times. With the Vietnam war as a backdrop, each story focuses on a different character in the neighborhood, and what their role was in raising or growing up with the main character, Taco. From Taco's Mami (mother, in Spanish), to their grandmother, Doña María, the matriarch based society in a community where the men rarely stayed is an interesting setting for a little boy to learn how to become a man. All the stories are like minute brush-strokes that give you the whole picture -- each story about one or two pages long. This makes for an easy and very quick read, and you can go through the entire book in pretty much just one sitting.

I enjoyed Taco, and the book reminded me of the foods, colors of Puerto Rico, and Puerto Rican friends of mine. I think that as a way to illustrate a culture and a piece of history of the United States, this is an interesting read.

WHAT READERS ARE SAYING ...

(cont) ...It does have some sordid details (a fairly graphic suicide), which makes it unsuitable for children, but the book is most definitely accessible for older teens and young adults. Mr. DeJesus is a new writer, and I believe he depicted the world he grew up in with a careful eye and a lot of emotion.

Erika G.

TACO

A Brooklyn Tale

John E. DeJesus

Visit TACO at:
http://www.TacoTheBook.com
E-Mail: tacothebook@yahoo.com

ISBN-10: 1979311099
ISBN-13: 978-1979311090

Library of Congress Cataloging-in-Publication has been applied for.
Library of Congress Control Number: 2011911922

Cover Art by: **Wook Jin Jung**
http://www.WookieStyle.com/
E-Mail: wookiemania@gmail.com
Please tell him that Taco sent you.

T.J.T.M.

Dedicated to "Mi Familia",

To **Mama Yeya**,

And to all the women

who never left.

TABLE OF CONTENTS

TACO

A Brooklyn Tale

MY NAME
IS TACO

They call me Taco. As far as nicknames go, I guess it's as good as any. But a Taco is ground-up corn meal, made into a shell and stuffed with meat and other spices. It's quite good, but it's a Mexican delicacy and I happen to be Puerto Rican. Using that same logic, I would have preferred to be called by a Puerto Rican food, like Relleno or maybe Empanada; but Taco it is.

The name came from a kid in the first grade. I remember the first day of class when the teacher asked us to stand up and tell the class a little about ourselves; our name and where we were from.

Just a few weeks ago we were boarding a plane from San Juan, Puerto Rico, where I was born. I was told it was a sunny day in Puerto Rico, but come to think about it, they were all mostly sunny. After all, it is a tropical island.

Before that first day in class, I used to look at the boxes of Ortega taco shells that Mami used to buy and be proud that our last name was on something popular; on something that brought joy to people. After all, who doesn't like eating tacos?

Anyway, I was standing in the front of the classroom with my hands in my pocket. I was so glad that my Mom insisted on speaking English in our house.

"I want you to grow up to be someone, and I don't want you to have a Spanish accent. You'll get more opportunities without it.", Mami would say.

"So Juan, where are you from?", asked Miss McAffee.

With all the courage I could: "Miss McAffee, I'm from Puerto Rico."

"Puerto Rico?", she continued, "That's a tropical island in the Caribbean."

"All I know is that it's hot!", I responded as everyone laughed.

"What's his last name?", Percy asked.

"Well Juan?", Miss McAffee asked as she looked at me over her glasses.

"My name is Juan. Juan Ortega.", I answered.

"You mean like a Taco!", Percy shouted.

As the class joined in on the laughter, I knew that Percy was going to be the thorn in my side.

From that day on, just about everyone called me "Taco". After a while I grew to like it. It made me unique. At least I wasn't one of two Juans.

ONE OF TWO JUANS

We lived on Wyckoff Street in Brooklyn. The block was a mixture of Brownstones and apartment buildings. We even had a bakery on one corner, and a Bodega directly across the street from it.

We lived in a white Brownstone. I should have realized that my life would be interesting from this very fact. It was the only white thing in our neighborhood. Sure, some of us were light-skinned, but none of us were considered white; and definitely not with our nappy hair. The whitest kid I knew was my friend, Juan Goldstein.

I guess we were drawn to each other because we both shared the same first name; but that's where the similarity ended. We were as different as two friends could be. I was Roman Catholic, along with ninety percent of my neighborhood, and he was a Puerto Rican Jew.

Juan was by far the lightest thing in our neighborhood, besides the building I lived in. For that very reason, he became known as Juan Blanco.

I, on the other hand, was closer to a tan color and became known as Juan Pardo; or at least until Percy made that Taco comment in First Grade. After that, Juan and I stopped having that one thing in common. Our friendship ended shortly after.

ROYALTY

Almost every adult in the neighborhood had a Title. It was either Don or Doňa, Tío or Tía, Suegra or Fulano de Tal. Never understood the last one, but I hear Fulano is well known. At least the older people had titles. I always thought it was because they were Royalty, but Mami said it was out of respect.

"You have to respect your elders.", Mami would always say.

I guess that's why it's Don Paco or Doňa María; it's Tío Alberto or Tía Nady. But I still like to think of them as Royalty. I know they dressed like royalty. The men wore a dress shirt called a guayabera, with slacks and shoes; almost like they dressed for church, but without the jacket. The women wore a dress or a blouse with a skirt; but always with shoes. They just loved their shoes.

So we know who to respect. If they have a title, then they are well respected. At least here on Wyckoff Street.

WYCKOFF STREET

Y ou could smell Wyckoff Street before you even turned the corner. The aroma just made your mouth water. It was all the Spanish food cooking and simmering, in pots and pans, inside apartments up and down the block. Even heated-up leftovers somehow smelled so much better on Wyckoff Street.

Maybe it wasn't the aroma itself, but the way we all pulled together to make our life here better. The Doñas had started a "Make Wyckoff Street Better" campaign years ago. And that's why when anyone asked where I lived, and I told them Wyckoff Street, they always responded with: "You mean the block with all the trees?"

It wasn't only the trees; it was that everyone took part in cleaning up the block, especially on Saturdays. That's when everyone would wake up early to clean in front of their buildings and stoops. It reminded me of those Olympic Games, where a bunch of people would do the same thing at the same time, and then the judges would vote. If I could vote here, I would have given everyone on Wyckoff Street a ten.

MOM AND HER SPIES

Even though our neighborhood was considered by many to be a dangerous place, none of us felt that way. I guess that's because we knew everyone, and everyone knew us. And we all looked out for each other.

Mami worked all day while Doña María, my grandmother, cared for us. Mami would know exactly where we were and what we did, each and every day. And she was very happy to let us know this.

"What were you doing on Fulton Street today?", she questioned. "Didn't I tell you no further than Court Street?"

"But Mami, there was a Dracula Festival downtown. They had Dracula, Son of Dracula, Blackula, Mulatto Son of Miss Dracula and Blackula...", I said as Mami interrupted.

"I don't care what was playing where; you don't go past Court Street. Punto y se acabo!", Mami exclaimed.

"Period and that's it!" was Mami's way of telling us that we had no choice.

"But Mami, how did you know?", I asked.

With a smirk she replied, "I have my spies."

I always wondered who her spies were. Was it Don Julio, who always brought us Spanish bread? Or was it Doňa Idalia, who made the best pasteles around? Or was it Doňa Rivera, who sold Limber de Leche, a frozen treat, from in front of her house? Maybe it was Don Paco, who sold snow cones, which we called Piraguas, in the summer and who was always yelling at his son Papo.

Whomever it was, Mami had good spies; probably better than the FBI or the CIA.

MAMI

Mami's real name was María, like her mom Doña María, but we called her Mami. Mami had long black hair, caramel brown eyes and soft white skin. Her hair wasn't as long as it used to be when she was younger. I saw pictures of Mami before Inez and José and me; before Wyckoff Street. And even before my father.

Mami looked like a Movie Star. In fact, Mami was in a few soap operas in Puerto Rico, until my father came along and swept her away. Mami's friend Jenny, who told Mami to stay in Puerto Rico, went on to become rich and famous. Mami instead left Puerto Rico with my father, and came to Wyckoff Street.

Mami always talked about all the fun she and Jenny had dressing up and acting. One time, Mami borrowed a movie camera from my uncle, Tío Alberto, and we filmed a scene; like in a movie. I remember Mami being excited, like she belonged there; when I knew all along that Mami belonged with us.

And Doña María helped by dressing us up in weird costumes, and going over our sentences, which she called "lines", and putting make-up on us.

"The lights are hot, so you need make-up to look good.", Doña María said.

I know Mami was beautiful because a lot of men buzzed around Mami, like real bees buzzed around beautiful flowers. I sometimes heard that Mami was so beautiful that she could stop a clock. I often wondered how Mami could do that, and how big that clock would have to be.

INEZ

Inez had black hair like Mami's, only Inez thought that her hair was too curly. She was always trying to brush it straight to look like Mami's hair. And when she did, Inez would count each time that she brushed: "One, two, three, four...".

Sometimes José and me would wait until Inez counted to a high number. And then we would go into her room, the one she shared with Mami, and yell out different numbers to confuse her. And Inez would start saying the wrong numbers and then chase us with her brush.

Inez was thin; so thin that she looked like those pipe things that we used in Miss McAffee's class, when we did art projects. Although they were called "pipe cleaners", I often wondered how many of these would you have to tie together in order to clean a pipe.

Inez was a year older than me, but the difference didn't matter. It seemed like we were the same age. Inez didn't like girlie things, like dolls and strollers and tea cups. She preferred snails and pails and puppy dog tails; the stuff I heard that boys were made of.

And whenever we played cops and robbers, she would always want to be the "Police Officer". Inez didn't like being called a "cop"; almost like she wanted a title or something.

But I think that Inez really wanted to be a dancer like Doña María. I know this because sometimes I would catch Inez practicing with Doña María; and Inez would smile a big smile. And not just a regular smile. She would smile a "Christmas Smile"; that smile where you opened your presents on Christmas Day, and you see that you got exactly what you had wished for.

JOSÉ

José was the baby of the family, only he wanted to be older. He wanted to do things when I did them; but Mami was always saying my baby this, and my baby that. And although José said he didn't like it, I knew that he did like it because he would get the giggles.

José was lighter in complexion. If I was chocolate milk, then he was vanilla cream. He and Mami approached the complexion of Juan Goldstein, but I think the Taíno Indian influence from Puerto Rico held them back.

José never let anything get to him, and was always happy to help in many ways. Whenever you asked José how he was doing, he would always answer: "Great!", even if he was having a really bad day.

José was a gentleman. He always liked to help the ladies. Whenever Mami came home, José would run down the stairs and help Mami with any bags that she was carrying. He also did the same for the Doñas whenever they came down the block carrying groceries; and although the Doñas would offer him money, José never took it.

José was my roommate. We used to share the sofa bed in the living room. Sometimes we used to catch fits of laughter, and Mami would yell at us. And the louder she yelled, the more we laughed; although we tried not to. That was probably the only time Mami yelled at us, that I could remember. And she probably did it because she had to wake up early for work, even before the sun came up.

DOŇA MARÍA

In Spanish, "abuela" means "grandma". My abuela was a thin, shapely, red-headed beauty, who definitely turned many men's heads in her day. I would guess that it was the reason why Don Julio would travel to the corner bakery, each and every morning, to bring us Spanish bread. I cannot tell you for sure, but I had my suspicions.

My abuela took care of us when Mami was off working long hours. I heard that my abuela was a dancer in Puerto Rico, and that she danced up a storm. I know this because they named a storm after her: Hurricane Maria.

I was proud because my abuela was Royalty: Doňa Maria. So I felt that one day her royalty would be passed on to us.

Doña Maria loved life and I heard many times, that life loved her too. She would often tell us that life was a gift from God, and since God gave it to us, only God could take it away.

It bothered her that she was an abuela. For that very reason, she insisted that we call her Doña Maria, just like everyone else. I think she was trying to fool God. Maybe God wouldn't take her away to Heaven if He knew she wasn't an abuela. I don't think Doña Maria realized that God seemed to claim a lot of Royalty.

DON JULIO

Don Julio lived across the street from us and each and every day, for as long as I could remember, he would go to the corner bakery and bring us Spanish bread. I think he may have worked for the Post Office because he had the same motto: "Neither snow, nor rain, nor heat ...".

We woke up every morning to the smell of Bustelo coffee and Spanish bread. Just the aroma of both was enough to make us jump out of our beds. We rushed into the kitchen to be greeted by Don Julio and his "Special Delivery". And to be treated to Don Julio's stories over breakfast; his adventures in the Army, and how he captured a bridge single-handedly.

We always thought Don Julio had a huge imagination, until we read his obituary the day after he died. It said that he had been awarded a Purple Heart, two Bronze Stars and the Congressional

Medal of Honor. It was then that Don Julio's stories took on new meaning; we now believed them.

I can still remember that day, the day Don Julio died. We awoke to Bustelo coffee, but something was missing. The smell of Spanish bread was gone. We rushed into the kitchen this time, but no Don Julio. The kitchen was empty. We rushed out the front door to the stoop, just in time to see them put the white covered stretcher into the back of a long black car.

And just like that, he was gone. No more Spanish bread. No more stories. No more smiles. And no more Don Julio.

OUT ON A LIMB

Me and Inez and José used to watch wrestling on television with my abuela, Doña Maria, and she used to really get into it. I mean as Doña Maria watched, she would sometimes use the moves she saw on us. One time Doña Maria placed me in a headlock, and she wouldn't let go until I gave up. And then she pranced around the room with her arms raised in victory.

Doña Maria used to take us to the park a lot. She would tell us that we needed to see more than parked cars, and sidewalks with gum on it. I remember one time we're in the park and Doña Maria hands Inez a camera. And she tells Inez to take a picture of her, once she was up in the tree.

I was so scared watching Doña Maria climb up that tree, and out onto the limb. So here we are yelling and screaming, trying to talk my abuela, I mean Doña Maria, down from a tree and she ignored us and continued up the tree.

Finally Doña Maria sits herself out on a branch and yells down to us: "Take the picture. Hurry up. Take the picture. I don't think this branch can hold me."

Inez took two pictures and then we watched Doña Maria make her way down the tree. I couldn't tell you how happy I was when Doña Maria's feet were back on solid ground.

DANCING
COOK

Doña Maria loved to dance and she loved to cook. And she loved both of them so much that she combined them. As the Spanish music played, Doña Maria danced and cooked, and the dancing would make her mix foods together. We always knew that once Doña Maria cooked to music, that we were not quite sure what we were going to get.

One time, during one of her cooking dances, she served us spaghetti with eggs. Another time we got rice with meatballs and beans. Truth be told, Inez and José and me liked it. It meant that Doña Maria thought enough of us to make us special meals.

And like clockwork, Doña Maria was always there to pick us up after school. Day in and day out, rain or shine. I think she learned that from the same school as Don Julio.

SNOW CONES

During the summer, people came from all around to buy snow cones. That delicious treat was a perfect refresher to top off a hot summer day. All the neighborhoods had different names for this addictive treat because, except for Wyckoff Street, all the other streets were mixtures of people from different countries.

People in Cuba called them granizados; whereas in the Dominican Republic, it was known as a frio-frio. In Mexico, Nicaragua and Colombia, they are called raspados, but Hondurans called it nieve. In El Salvador, it's a minuta and in Guatemala, a charamusca.

But here, here on Wyckoff Street, we called them Piraguas. And when the Piraguas man, or Piraguero, used to come down the block, all the kids would run home to their buildings, and their Moms would throw down change.

Most of the time, the kids would miss the change and it would bounce on the sidewalk. And then the kids had to scramble to pick up the change before the Piraguero went on his merry way.

The best thing about eating a Piragua was not only that it cooled you off under the heat of the summer sun, but that it brought back sweet memories. Memories of Puerto Rico; the island, its people, and the sweet sounds of summer there.

BEES

One thing that always bothered me was that, although there were many men in our neighborhood, not too many of them stayed with their families; at least not the younger ones. Maybe that's why when they saw each other, they used to say: "Yo bees."

It was like the men were bees, and they would go from flower to flower; and then they would move on. They never stayed around to care for their wives or their kids. I think they thought that having a lot of kids made them a man. But I think not running away and watching over your kids made you a man.

The heads of our families were the women. The Moms never left. They never ran away. They would take one, two, maybe three jobs. And they would work until their feet hurt. And they wouldn't sleep much. And they would leave the house before the sun went up in the morning, and come back after the sun went down.

I didn't want kids. I didn't want to leave them crying and alone. I didn't want to make my wife work until her feet hurt, and she cried herself to sleep. Don Paco was one of the only men on our block who stayed with his family, but I think maybe it was because he was *Royalty*.

NO SENSE

In life, a lot of things just don't make any sense; even in church they don't. The last shall be first, and the first shall be last. Or that bit about getting a camel to go through the eye of a needle. Now I've never seen a camel up close, only in pictures in Miss McAffee's class, but I have seen a needle. And I don't think that one hair on a camel's head could fit through the eye of the needle, let alone the whole camel.

Mami had no one but Inez and José and me. And Don Paco had no wife. So why couldn't Don Paco be younger or Mami older? Then they would have each other, and I would have been Papo's brother. And Don Paco could pass on the Piraguas cart to me.

But so far, everything I see makes no sense. Like, why did my father leave Mami? I see how men look at Mami, and how they talk to her.   But they don't want kids; these men that look at my Mom. They're the same ones that buzz like bees.

And Mami; well she's still hoping my father would return someday. Maybe one day God will show me the way. Although I hope He doesn't send me that camel riddle; at least not until I'm a *Don.*

FELIZ NAVIDADES

I always thought everyone had them - two "Christmases" or "Navidades". It really surprised me to learn that people who didn't live on Wyckoff Street had only one Christmas - on December 25th.

Here on Wyckoff Street, we also celebrated Christmas on January 6th. That was the day when Los Tres Reyes Magos - the three Wise Men - paid a visit to baby Jesus and made him a gifted child.

We would put hay under the Christmas tree for the camels; the same camels that did that trick of going through the eye of a needle. Maybe that's why those camels brought kings to see Jesus, because the camels had special powers. And the kings needed to see their boss. After all, Jesus was the King of kings.

Although we didn't get as many gifts on the second Christmas as we got on the first Christmas, Mami always made sure to give us something. And to us, it was known as 'little Christmas'.

And we celebrated this day with song and dance. And we ate pasteles all over again; those pasteles, which we had made to celebrate Christmas, were brought out again and re-heated.

To me, having two birthdays made Jesus extra special. I mean, He deserved it. After all, Jesus said "I Love You this much!", and He opened His arms up and died.

LA
MADAMA

Mami never hit us but whenever she wanted to punish us, she would always say: "La Madama te va a cojer!" That meant "the Madama was going to get you." And we instantly got scared and stopped what we were doing and listened.

The way Mami described her, La Madama was dark like the night and was dressed all in red. She looked like the same woman that was on the syrup jar, only la Madama flew on a broom.

So when we were bad, Mami would say: "La Madama te va a cojer!", and it seemed to work; especially when we did something late at night. We ended up being so scared that we pulled up the covers, so that only our noses stuck out.

And for the rest of the night we worried, wondering when La Madama was going to come and get us.

Mami said La Madama liked to take away bad children on her broom, and make them work on her farm until they were good.

EL HOMBRE DE PIRAGUAS

Don Paco lived upstairs from us and sold Piraguas. I guess that was his job and as funny as it sounds, I wanted it to be my job too. Don Paco was a hero to me. He would walk up and down the street selling his delicious treat of sweet colored ice to everyone; adult or child, husband or wife, friend or foe. We all liked Piraguas. We all liked Don Paco and his frozen treat. And I too, wanted to sell Piraguas when I grew up.

In this neighborhood, you grew up to work with your hands; to clean toilets and sinks, to pick up trash, to be a super of a building or to sell Piraguas. I figured if I had to do anything, I would have preferred to bring some joy into the world; and make some money doing it.

Don Paco would come home every day with his pockets full of cash; more cash than I had ever seen. I knew this because he would pay me to wash his Piraguas Cart. And I was glad to do it.

I thought I could work my way up; maybe he would make me his helper. Maybe, just maybe.

And then one day it happened. I asked Don Paco to show me how to make a Piragua, and he did. He showed me how to scrape the ice with the special ice shaver machine. I thought that it was going to be a marvel of science at first, but he showed me it was just a metal box, with a blade that caught the ice shavings as you moved it across the block of ice. And the special flavors; just corn syrup he got from huge jars that he poured into the bottles using a funnel. Not much to making one.

The hard part was walking up and down the street, day in and day out. Don Paco soaked his feet every night because he walked so much. Everyone made fun of him. Me, I wanted to sell Piraguas. And now that I knew his secrets, I knew I could do the job.

A FRIEND
IN DEED

Actions speak louder than words. What you do for the least of my brothers, you do for me. A friend in need is a friend indeed. That's how it was on Wyckoff Street. When something bad happened, we all pulled together to help each other; whether it was by collecting money, or collecting food or clothes. We all got together like one big crazy family.

Sure, we argued, yelled, threw things at each other; whether they were insults or objects. But when the chips were down, all the differences were put aside to help the neighbor in need. We would get together at that person's house to help out in any way; big or small. And we always called in the Royalty: the Dons and the Doñas. They were the wise ones, and they always had the answers.

I guess that dressing up all the time gave you magical powers, so as you got older, you dressed nicer and became wiser.

I always wondered if I was the only one who figured it out, or maybe it was written in a book somewhere. It didn't matter; I was planning to be Royalty selling Piraguas ... *Don Juan.*

THE LADY IN HOT PANTS

They used to watch her bounce down the street, the lady next door, in her hot pants. She was young enough not to have a "Royal Title", but old enough to be a widow already. A lot of men tried to talk to her. I heard that they wanted to get into her hot pants. But she just loved to listen to music and dance, and drink liquids from long stemmed glasses.

And the more she drank, the more she cried. I used to watch her, ever since I climbed the tree that faced her back yard, and caught a glimpse of her. I would watch her dance and cry and fall asleep, and then get up and take a shower.

Once, when she was getting dressed, she turned to the mirror and saw me in the reflection. I know this because then she quickly turned around and looked directly at me. I tried to hide, but there was only so much you can hide out on the limb of a tree.

Later, after I had finally come down from the tree, I went into the front yard. There she was, the woman in hot pants, talking to Mami; only she was wearing a dress. I was frozen with fear, until Mami called out my name.

"Juan, please come here for a minute.", Mami said.

I tell you that my heart must have beaten one hundred times for each step that I took. And when I finally reached Mami: "Juan, this is Ms. Rosado. Ms. Rosado, this is my son Juan."

"Please to meet you young man. You're quite a handsome fellow.", she said as she bent down to shake my hand.

I still remember how the touch of her hand made me tingle inside.

"Juan," Mami continued, "Ms. Rosado asked me if it was okay to have you help her clean out her basement, and she'll pay you too. So would you like to make some money? Huh Juan?".

I couldn't believe what I was hearing. I kept thinking it was a dream beginning but with a nightmare ending. That at any moment Ms. Rosado would spill the beans about the watchful eye I kept on her from that tree.

In the weeks that followed, Ms. Rosado had me work a lot. She would even let me take naps on her big comfortable bed. Sometimes she would lie down next to me and talk, but not too close.

One time when I woke up from a nap, I was wrapped up in her arms. She began to kiss me and it felt so good, until I felt her tongue in my mouth. I was so scared that I jumped up. That's when I decided to stop working for Ms. Rosado.

I wasn't mad at her at all. I just didn't know what to do next, but I bet it had to do with getting into her hot pants.

But every once in a while, I would climb up into that tree, and she would put on a show for me.

THE WATCHFUL
EYE OF PAPO

All the kids loved Papo. He was older, but he was like one of us who never really grew up. Papo was fun to be with. He would make us laugh or show us tricks or tell us jokes. Papo was also our guardian; our big brother.

Papo was like a sheep dog tending to his flock. And he always kept a watchful eye out for us as he sat on the stoop, blasting Spanish music from his "Boom Box". I didn't quite know how he could be listening to music, dancing, talking to the honeys and still be watching over us; but he did.

Once an old man pulled up to Carmen and tried to yank her into the car. Papo was off the stoop in seconds. He yanked the man out of the car and beat him badly. It was the police who actually saved the man because the neighborhood watched Papo give the man what he deserved.

Of course Papo went to jail. I think the police locked Papo up because he knew too much. After that day, no cars came down our block looking for trouble. The only cars that drove down our block were the ones that belonged on the block, or who were passing by with their doors locked and windows rolled up.

It wasn't in the paper but everyone knew. The word must have gotten around. They knew that if you came down our block and messed with any of our kids, that Papo was going to get you.

WISDOM

Every Sunday, we went to Church whether we wanted to or not; Mami always made sure of it. Mami told us that God was always watching over us, and we needed to go see Him, so He wouldn't forget us. Some people never wanted to be forgotten because they were always at Church. Usually, it was the Dons and the Doñas who went to Church a lot.

Maybe that's why they had all the answers. Maybe God talked to them and gave them all the answers they needed. I know they always said that. Maybe God was there to help us deal with those bad times, because nothing ever stopped those bad times from coming.

Once I asked Papo to come with me to Church, but he refused. Never really knew why; after all, he was once an altar boy. I think he may have been given too much wisdom too early, and it scared him off.

Maybe that's why he ran around, had no job, and drank a little too much sometimes. And he and Don Paco used to fight a lot. Don Paco always wanted Papo to do something with his life; to sell Piraguas like him. I didn't know why Papo didn't want to do it. I mean with the wisdom and the Piraguas cart, I think Papo could have been one of the youngest Dons in our neighborhood.

I always hoped that Don Paco would pass the job over to me. After all, Papo was refusing and Don Paco had no one to pass the Piraguas business to. And we definitely couldn't go without a Piraguas cart; especially not in the summer. Not on Wyckoff Street.

$\mathcal{HOPE}$

Mami and Papo were friends; and although I had always hoped that they would become more, I knew it would never work out. Papo was too much like a kid; Papo was playful and fun loving. While Mami was always hoping that my father would someday return; that my father would make our lives easier. And that my father would make us laugh and smile and dream; dream of better things and a better life. Mami said my father was a good man, but I had heard this before.

"If he's such a good man, where is he?", I would ask. "We are struggling. Where is our father?"

Mami really didn't know what to answer, but made some excuse about how he was young and we were too much for him. But me, I didn't think that he would ever come back.

Sure, fathers came back every once in a while, but they never brought any happiness. The family was usually worse off with him, than without him. And the family cried and feared and was sad. And the father bullied and drank and hit. I knew we were better off.

Just Mami and Inez and José and me... *The Ortegas.*

DON
REYES

Don Reyes lived down the block from us and like Don Julio, he went to war; to fight for the United States and to keep this country brave and free.

Don Reyes would sit in his front yard at his domino table waiting for someone to come by to get a domino game going, so he could talk a lot. I always liked passing by and playing dominoes with Don Reyes. He had a lot of wisdom, and I liked that he passed that wisdom on to me.

I think this is how you become a Don; by listening to the Dons and the Doñas and using their wisdom whenever you needed it. Just like in Cub Scouts, when you learn stuff so you can "be prepared" in case of an emergency that you hope would never come; or just in case something else happened.

I thought I had heard that Don Reyes was a pirate in the Army because he said he was one of the "Borinqueneers" in the Korean War. It reminded me of that character, in a pirate movie, who takes over an old ship, and then fights with a sword and wins. I wondered how many times Don Reyes swung on a rope, or fought with a sword. And if that's how he and Don Julio got so many medals.

I'm not sure, but I think that one time I had seen Don Reyes on TV marching with other people against that 'Nam war. It looked like Don Reyes, but I thought why would he fight in one war and then complain about another?

Maybe it was because whenever Don Reyes showed me his medals, and the pictures of the friends that he said he left behind there, he would cry. I never asked Don Reyes, but I often wondered why would he leave his friends there? And how come they never came back?

BORN TO DANCE

Dancing was important on Wyckoff Street. We all had to dance, or at least be able to learn to. The Dons and the Doňas used to say that Puerto Ricans were born dancing. They said that we all had rhythm, but some of us forgot somewhere along the line; just like some of us forgot to speak Spanish.

The Dons and the Doňas used to say that dancing was the Spanish way to celebrate: to celebrate our life, to be thankful to God, and to know that no matter what happened in life, that dancing would make it better.

The Dons and the Doňas used to have dancing parties to teach anyone to get the "dancing bug" in them to come out. We would meet at Don Julio's house and everyone would move Don Julio's furniture around so that there was nothing left in his living room, but the wooden floor.

Then Doña Maria would show everyone how to dance. She would shake her hips and spin fast, and move her feet even faster. And her and Don Julio would show everyone the right way to move. Sometimes they moved slow, and sometimes they moved fast.

Doña Maria used to say: "The music will tell you how to move. Let the music move your hips and everything will follow."

And she was right. I know whenever the ladies moved their hips, that the men would look at them and follow them with their eyes. And the better the women's hips moved, the more the men's mouths stayed open; almost like when someone shows you something that's amazing.

But I think that dancing was another way to make things better on Wyckoff Street. That even though we were here, away from our "Isla Bonita", that we could bring back sweet memories of our "Beautiful Island" and its people. That we could listen to the music until it moved us and brought us back to **Puerto Rico.**

EN MI VIEJO
SAN JUAN

Music was also a big part of our lives, just like dance; whether Mami played records or Papo played the radio. Or the Dons and the Doñas played the drums, the cymbals, the tambours or the maracas; on their front stoops.

It was the rhythm in the music that made Puerto Ricans dance, move and celebrate. No matter how bad things would get, music would always cheer us up, and for a little while, make us happy enough to want to go on. I heard that the music was passed on to us from the early Taíno Indians, so we had to make sure to pass it on too.

But there was one song, that no matter who played it or when it was played, that touched every Puerto Rican's heart; especially the Dons and the Doñas. That song was: "En Mi Viejo San Juan" (In My Old San Juan).

Whenever that song played, everyone on Wyckoff Street sang, and you could see people's eyes water up with tears. And they would stand taller.

Don Julio once told me that the song is a story about a man who leaves his heart in Puerto Rico. And the man says that it's only for a little while, but he will be back soon to get it. But Father Time laughs at him because people never realize how fast time really does go by. And before the man knows it, his hair is white and he's close to death, but he's still missing his heart; the one he left on the shores of Puerto Rico. And the man doesn't want to die without his heart or away from Puerto Rico.

I know that it's one of those riddles that you need to be a Don to understand, but it doesn't stop me from feeling sad. I think that Don Julio was talking about himself. And I think that somewhere deep down, even though we left Puerto Rico and came to Wyckoff Street, that Puerto Rico never left us. And our hearts are still there, on that sandy shore, watching the sun sink into the sea ... *waiting for us to return.*

PAPI IS
BACK

One day I'm coming home from school, and as I get to the stoop in front of my house, a man tells me that he's my father. I get a little scared, until I see Papo come down the stairs. They say something to each other in Spanish and Papo walks upstairs and knocks on my front door, but still keeps a watchful eye on me.

Mami comes down the stairs and is surprised to see my father. Mami tells me to go inside and I do. And through the window, I saw them not quite arguing, but not quite having a calm discussion. Later on that evening, my father had dinner with us and Mami introduced us to him.

"This is your Papi.", Mami said.

I didn't really know just how to feel. It felt weird to know that I had a father all along. Papi wanted to make up for the lost time, and he did try. In those few months, it looked like we were going to be a family: Mami and Papi, my sister Inez and my brother José and me.

Papi took us to Yankee Stadium in the Bronx, and to the zoo. He took us to the park, and to the movies. Mami was happy. We were eating good and we were laughing and smiling and dancing.

Papi became friends with Papo, and sometimes they went out together. Maybe now that they were friends, Papo and Papi, I could have Papi talk to Papo to talk to Don Paco. Life seemed to be going well. That Piraguas cart was well within my grasp.

EL REGALO

So one day we're sitting at home and a feeling comes over me. My eyes are closed, but I can see clear as day as someone climbs into our bathroom window, and searches our apartment. And the robber takes our stuff and Doña Maria's jewelry.

I open up my eyes and I tell Mami and Papi. Papi doesn't believe me, but the look in Mami's eyes tells me that she believes every word of it.

"He has visions of things before they happen. Taco can see the future.", Mami says.

"How can he see the future?", Papi continues, "He's just a kid!"

"He did it before.", Mami answers. "El tiene el Regalo."

"Okay Taco, if you 'have the Gift', then impress me. Tell me the winning lottery numbers.", Papi says.

"Papi, I can't do that.", I said. "It just happens."

"Nothing just happens. It don't work like that.", Papi says. "Now tell me the winning lottery numbers.", he says as he grabs my arm.

"Let him go right now!", Mami says, as she pulls me away and gives me a hug.

"You know, you baby him too much. He should be making us money. Maybe have Taco read people's Tarot cards.", Papi says.

"He's going to be something. Something that's bigger than us or Wyckoff Street. Maybe a doctor or a lawyer? Or maybe even a judge?", Mami says proudly.

"He's gonna be nothing; like he is now. No one gets out of this neighborhood. No one!", Papi says as he storms out of the house.

When Papi finally comes home, he catches a robber, just as the robber is sneaking out of our house with our stuff. And Papi beats the robber up and breaks his leg. The police come and take the bad man away. And Mami turns to Papi and says: *"El tiene el regalo. He has the gift."*

NO MORE JUMPING ON THE BED

The house was decorated with balloons and streamers, and all the fancy stuff they use at parties. José woke me up as he always did on everyone's birthday and said: "If you don't get up now, you won't get any of your birthday cake." And as usual, I hit him on the head with a pillow.

Mami told us to get up for breakfast and after that, she had me dress up in a suit.

"But Mami, why do I have to get dressed up like I'm going to church?", I said.

"It's your birthday. Everyone dresses up for their birthday. Don't you want to look good in the pictures?", Mami said.

"Aw Mami.", I answered.

"Don't 'Aw Mami me'. Get dressed. You'll get more presents that way.", Mami said.

Me and José and Inez got dressed and Mami made me stand in front of the birthday table. And she took a few pictures of me.

"You should always take pictures when you're happy.", Mami said, "So when you look back, you can remember the good times and forget the bad ones."

Mami and Inez went to the bodega on the corner, while me and José sat in the living room. But it was boring sitting around dressed in a suit, so me and José decided to go jump on the bed. I figured since we were standing up while we were jumping, we wouldn't mess up our church clothes.

A BAD BREAK

Papi told us not to jump on the bed; he had already yelled at us a couple of times. Papi had gotten home early in the morning, after a night out with Papo. He and Mami had an argument and Papi was lying on the couch. Mami went with Inez to pick up some candles that Papi forgot to get.

So here we were having fun jumping on the bed and we didn't listen to Papi the first two times; but I knew we would listen on the third time, if only Papi had given us a chance. There was no chance.

The bedroom door flew open and Papi stepped through the door, and he reached out. It was my birthday, so he grabbed me. And he hit me. He hit me hard with his big boot; the one he wore to his Security Guard job. And I cried. And then it happened; I heard a snap.

I began to scream so loud that Mami heard me from the corner bodega. Mami ran home and up the stairs as quickly as she could to reach me.

"What did you do!", Mami screamed.

Papi called for an ambulance, but Mami knew better; especially in this neighborhood. Instead, she called a car service. The car service came first and Mami carried me downstairs. We got into the car service and rushed to the hospital. The doctor at the hospital put my leg in a cast and Mami called the car service again and we went home.

As the car service got closer to Wyckoff Street, we saw a lot of fire engines and police cars; and there was smoke coming from our block. Since we couldn't get any closer, the car service let us out around the block. Me and Mami got out and started to walk and, as we turned the corner, we saw that our building had been on fire.

I can't forget looking up to the second floor, the floor we lived on, and seeing a fireman breaking the glass and dropping down a burnt smoking mattress. Mami was crying.

In the span of one day, our lives had changed again. I hated my father. I hated him for coming back and for making us love him. I hated him for taking care of us and making Mami smile. And I hated him for taking it all away.

TÍO ALBERTO

After the fire, we went to live with my uncle, Tío Alberto. Mami said we would probably stay two weeks. They had to fix up the apartment on Wyckoff Street and paint it.

Mami was happy that we were all okay, Inez and José and me; even though we lost everything. Mami said that maybe we needed a new start, and it was always good to have a new start.

Tío Alberto was a funny man who used to sing Spanish songs. His wife, Tía Hermenia, loved to cook. I mean every meal was a big occasion; I guess it was because they had six kids. I knew Tía Hermenia loved to cook because she was always in the kitchen.

Tío Alberto used to tell us stories about Puerto Rico, and the nights sitting on the beach watching the sun "sink into the sea". And he told us about the frog in Puerto Rico, called the "coqui", and how it was always calling out its own name.

And he showed us how to play dominoes, which was a big thing in Puerto Rico. No one could beat Tío Alberto, but I did once. And I think he let me win because I had a cast on my leg.

Tío Alberto was so much fun to be with, but I think it was because he was always drinking. Every time we would see Tío Alberto, he would be going into, coming out of, or sitting in the corner bar. We would watch Tío Alberto, through the bar's window, telling stories to the people inside. And they would laugh and smile and would want him to stay.

And Tío Alberto would always say: "Uno mas." "One more" meant he would have just one more drink and leave; but he would continue telling stories. And my cousins, who we called primos, would end up going into the bar to get Tío Alberto for dinner.

I guess we were just like the people inside of the bar. We always wanted to hear one more story. I don't think it was the story itself, but the way Tío Alberto told it. He would make faces and act the story out; like he was on stage somewhere. Mami told me that Tío Alberto was an actor in Puerto Rico, but then he met Tía Hermenia and came to New York.

BACK TO
WYCKOFF

It took almost a month, but we made it back to Wyckoff Street. The day that we got back, Wyckoff Street gave us a block party. The Dons and the Doñas were dressed up like they did on Sunday for Church.

We left the subway, Mami and Inez and José and me, and walked to the corner and saw the street blocked off. I was worried that something else had happened, like another fire, until I saw Don Paco with his Piraguas cart.

"Bienvenido Taco. Welcome Back." Don Paco continued, "We've been waiting for you. Everyone did this to welcome you back. We missed you."

As the crowd gathered around us, I ran into Don Paco's arms and gave him a big hug.

"And the Piraguas are free!", said Don Paco.

"Then I will take two.", said José as we all laughed.

Don Paco had a pig roasting on a metal bar in an oil drum. The drum had been cut open and it had charcoal on the bottom of it. Don Paco cooked the pig until the 'pernil', or 'pork' fell off the bone. I know he was an expert at it because he even had a metal net to catch any meat that fell off without his knowledge.

And the Doñas made 'arroz con gandules', or 'rice with pigeon peas.' And Doña Idalia made pasteles, like she made for the two Christmases. And Papo rented a truck that had a swing ride in it. And Papo sat next to Mami and we all rode together on one side. Mami and Papo sat on top and José and Inez and me sat on the bottom; like a real family.

And we all had fun. People played dominoes and they ate. The girls jumped rope and they ate. And we played stoop ball and stick ball, and we ate. It was like Thanksgiving, only the guests were the size of Wyckoff Street and the table was the size of a block.

EL TÍO

Things seemed to be getting worse for us. Mami never said anything, but I used to watch her through half-open doors, crying herself to sleep and praying to God and all the saints she kept on her dresser.

Mami had a friend named Blanca, who got her into Santeria. In Santeria, you asked the Saints to speak to God so that God could help you. Blanca would visit us every once in a while, but Doña Maria never liked her. Doña Maria always said that you could only pray to God and His Son Jesus for help. And no one else had powers here on earth; so I didn't believe in these things, but Mami started to.

Blanca always wore white, like she was going to a wedding, and had all these colored beads hanging from her neck. Mami would go see "El Tío", which is what everyone called him.

El Tio was a santero. A santero is a priest for poor people. When the real church doesn't want to listen, I hear a santero does.

I never really knew "The Uncle's" real name, but I heard he was so powerful that the very mention of his name could cause havoc, so everyone called him "El Tío". I remember Mami taking me along to talk to El Tío. She was hoping that our luck would change, but I didn't believe him. He would just take what little money Mami had, and give her these strong smelling potions to put here and there and wait.

Now how could this guy, who lives in an apartment just like us, have special powers? Shouldn't El Tío live in a palace with everything he knew? From what I heard, El Tío was always playing the numbers, but he would never win. And everyone said it was because he could only help others and not himself. I didn't believe it because if that were true, then why would he even play in the first place? You would think El Tío would know better.

Me, I just think El Tío knew how to read people. Just like Tío Alberto used to do when he played poker and he would tell me who was going to do what, just by how they looked or what they said.

PAPI IS STILL HERE

So one day I run home from playing, just to get a drink of water. Usually, I would get my water from the faucet in front of our building, but Don Paco was washing his Piraguas cart.

Anyway, I called out and I guess Mami didn't hear me, but I heard them. Mami and Papo were kissing in the bedroom; I could see them through the crack of the door. I was so happy that it made me start to think of Papo becoming my father, and then Don Paco would be my grandfather, or whatever you call it.

And then it happened; somehow Papi's picture fell over. Mami jumped up, picked up the picture and stared at it.

Then Mami said: "This is no good. It's a sign."

"But Maria, I'm here and he's not. He left you.", said Papo.

"We left him.", Mami answered.

"What does it matter who left who?" Papo continued, "Where was he when José was sick with a high fever and you woke me up at three in the morning and we ran to the hospital because we couldn't get a cab? Or when Inez fell off her bike and broke her arm? Huh? Where? And how about Taco's birthday? Did you forget?", Papo asked.

"Look Papo, I thank you for everything; I really do. I know I could never repay you.", said Mami.

Papo continued, "I'm not asking you for payback. Can't you see I love you? And I love the kids too. We could be a real family."

Then Mami said: "You're living in a fantasy world Papo! You want a family and you can't even take care of yourself. How are we going to live because we certainly can't live on love!"

"Now who's living in a fantasy world? You keep staring at that picture of him like he's coming back when you should know damn well he's not. He's long gone! Probably has another family by now." Papo continued, "And you're here wishing he comes back. You know what? I'm done with you. If the kids need anything, I'm there. But as for you, I'm done!"

And just like that, Papo stormed out of the room and past me. There was silence and then me and Mami looked at each other and cried. After that day, Mami and Papo were different. There were no more whispers when I was around. Just silence. Pure silence.

And I wasn't mad at Mami or Papo. I was mad at my father. Even though he was long gone, Papi was still hurting us.

I couldn't help thinking why I didn't listen to Papi that day, when he told me to stop jumping on the bed. If only I had listened.

DOŇA MARIA
IS GONE

Just like with Don Julio, there was one day that wasn't quite right. See Inez and José and me would wait by the school doors, and then exit together. We did this so that we would all rush to Doňa Maria, and hug her at the same time. But today, when we rushed out, we only saw Mami with red watery eyes and a worried look on her face.

"Mami, what are you doing here?", José asked.

"Yeah, where's Doňa Maria?", added Inez.

"Mami, where is Abuela?", I said.

Mami knelt down and reached out to hug us as she told us: "Kids, I'm so sorry but Doňa Maria passed away."

José stepped back, "Passed away to where? Where did she go?"

"Kids, Doňa Maria is in Heaven with Don Julio.", Mami said.

I couldn't help wondering if God was getting tired of the cooking up in Heaven, and needed to spice things up. Maybe God needed someone to dance while they cooked for Him. Maybe He needed to feel special again; it's hard to feel special when the people you love are dying. After all, there was a war going on in that 'Nam place, and good people were going there and good people were dying.

I still think back to that night; the night we had to dress in our church clothes and go see Doňa Maria. See Doňa Maria as she lay sleeping in that box that everyone called a casket. But I wasn't fooled, I knew what it was. I knew it was a fancy refrigerator that they laid down sideways. That's why Abuela felt so cold when I touched her. And that's the only way I could think of to keep the bodies fresh, so that God could make them rise up at the end of the world.

I cried a lot that night. And so did Mami and Inez and José. I cried for selfish reasons. No more special meals, no more wrestling, no more talking my abuela, I mean Doňa Maria, down from a tree and no more group hugs after school. The only thing that made me feel better was that our loss was God's gain. I know this because all the Dons and Doňas were in their Sunday best.

GOD'S PLAN

Mami had a friend named Magda. Didn't really know what her real name was because everyone called her Magda. It was like me with the name Taco. It stuck with me, so I guess it stuck with her.

So one day, we go to her apartment and she makes us grilled cheese sandwiches. I had never had one before, but I liked them instantly. After that day, it seemed that all I ever wanted to eat were grilled cheese sandwiches.

Mami would say: "You know, if you keep on like this, one day you'll turn into a grilled cheese."

"He looks like a cheese head now.", joked Inez.

And so whenever I had a choice, I always asked for a grilled cheese sandwich.

Magda had a baby recently and Mami stopped by to bring her some blankets and baby stuff. Magda had two sons and a daughter, like Mami; but with the new baby, she now had one more.

Magda's kids were fun to play with, but they didn't come out a lot. They were too busy taking care of each other, while Magda went out to find a father for them. Not even the baby's father stayed around to see the baby be born; he was another one of those bees.

Then one day, we saw smoke coming out of Magda's apartment window and fire engines racing down the block. And we all watched as the Firemen carried Magda's kids down the fire engine ladder, one by one. The baby they carried down wrapped up in a white blanket and they loaded her into that black car that came to pick up dead people. And Mami cried.

Everyone including the Policemen and Firemen cried for that baby. And the Police kept asking the kids where their mom was, as they sat on the edge of the fire engine, wrapped in blankets and breathing out of tubes.

I heard that Magda's kids were trying to make a grilled cheese sandwich because they were hungry, and accidentally set the apartment on fire. They were all found together in the baby's crib holding each other. Magda was arrested when she finally got home for being a bad mother and not taking care of her kids.

At the funeral, I asked Mami if the baby would become an angel because she wasn't here long enough to do anything bad, and Mami said yes. And the priests talked about God's will and that He had a plan.

So what was God's plan? Did he need more Angels in heaven like Doňa Maria and Don Julio? Why the baby? If the baby was going to die so soon, why was she born in the first place?

I wanted to know what God's plan was for me. Was I going to die making a grilled cheese? Would I ever own a Piraguas cart? Would I ever be wise enough to be a Don? And when I was that wise, would God let me know what His plan was?

I watched as Magda's kids sat in the front row and cried. I cried too for the baby girl. I cried for the kids. But most of all, I cried because I was happy I wasn't them, and I thought God would be mad at me.

THE GYPPER

After school we would always stop by Ibby's Candy Store. For a nickel, you could get all kinds of candy; from fish to buttons to sour styxs and everything in between. On the weekends, we would go and collect bottles and trade them in at the corner bodega for money. Or we would do chores on the block for the Dons or the Doñas; or anyone who had work for us to earn extra candy money.

But you had to be careful to watch your money when you went into Ibby's store because Ibby was a gypper. He liked to cheat people out of money; especially the young kids. One time, I had a bag of candy, and I put my money on the counter. And when I went to walk out, Ibby said that I didn't pay. I told him that I did but he said I didn't and took the candy away from me. My friends backed me up, but Ibby wasn't having it.

"Get out of my store now. You buy, you pay. That's the way." was all Ibby said.

I was so annoyed that I went home and told Mami. Mami dragged me and José and Inez to Ibby's Candy Store.

"Excuse me, are you trying to steal candy from my son?", Mami said.

"He took candy and didn't pay. You buy, you pay. That's the way." was all Ibby said.

Mami turned to me, "Taco, did you pay for the candy? Look at me and tell me the truth."

"Mami, I put the money right there on the counter.", I answered.

Mami turned to Ibby the gypper and said: "There you go."

"There goes nothing.", Ibby answered, "No money, no candy. You buy, you pay. That's the way."

"Let me tell you something Mr. Gypper, these are my kids. You see them?", Mami said as she pointed to us. Mami continued, "I work hard and they don't lie and they don't steal; but you stole from my son. If you don't give my son his candy, I am going to tell everyone in the neighborhood, everyone that I know, how you took money from a child." Mami continued, "I'll even stand outside every day with signs. And no one will come back here again. Do you understand me?".

Ibby looked at Mami and knew she meant business, so he gave each of us, José and Inez and me, a bag of candy.

Mami took away the bags from José and Inez, and gave it back saying, "Thank you, but my son only paid for one bag."

When we left the store, Mami explained, "Don't ever let anyone take away something that belongs to you. You stand up for what you want and you fight for what you believe in. You understand? Now please share the candy with your brother and sister."

After that, I don't think Ibby ever gypped anyone; at least not Mami or José or Inez or me.

NO
FIGHTING

One day I'm leaving school and even though Mami told me not to take my bike to school, I still did. I thought it would be cool.

So Hector Diaz comes up to me and starts looking at my bike. I know Hector because I really liked his sister, Maritza. It didn't help that Hector was also the class bully. That made a union between me and Maritza nearly impossible. Almost like that camel through the eye of the needle trick.

Anyway, Hector asks me if he can have a ride on my bike. I know that I shouldn't let him, but then he adds: "I'll let you walk my sister Maritza home from school." I was so excited that I didn't hear anything for about a minute because that's how long it took for Hector and his crew to disappear with my bike, and my date with Maritza.

I was angry at myself for taking the bike to school, and even angrier at myself for not listening to Mami. I know I wouldn't be able to hide this mess for long; especially not with all of Mami's spies running around.

So I walk home and on the way home, I see Don Reyes.

"What's troubling you son?", Don Reyes asks.

"Nothing.", I say.

But Don Reyes is too wise; it's that royalty thing.

"Taco, que te pasa? What's wrong? You can tell me.", he says.

And with that, I begin to spill the beans; until there aren't any more beans to spill.

"Well mi hijito, you can go and ask him for the bike. I'm sure he's reasonable.", Don Reyes says.

"You don't understand Don Reyes, he likes to beat people up. He does that a lot.", I explain.

"That's not true. No one likes to fight. Fighting is never good. No one ever wins in a fight.", Don Reyes says.

I'm confused because Don Reyes always talks about the war. The only thing I can think of is that maybe the war took the fight out of him. So I thank him for the advice and go on my merry way, thinking he may have a point. At least it doesn't hurt to try.

BIKE TROUBLE

So I'm on the floor with a bloody nose, watching Hector prance around after he just sucker punched me. And in an instant, I knew Don Reyes' plan failed miserably. Maybe it would have worked if I were in an Army uniform.

As I look around, I see that me and Hector are surrounded by kids yelling for us to fight. Hector yells at me to get up, but I'm frozen and can't hear anything. Suddenly I hear a clap of thunder and everything comes back: the chants, the sounds and the sight of blood on my shirt.

"This bike is mine. You gave it to me. You said you would trade it for a date with my sister.", Hector said.

And before I could say anything, lightning struck again; but this time it shot through my heart. Hector stepped aside and

I saw Maritza, standing next to him, with an embarrassed look on her face.

And all the kids were chanting: "Taco and Maritza sitting in a tree. K - I - S - S - I - N - G. First comes love. Then comes marriage. Then comes a baby in a baby carriage!"

Hector grabbed Maritza and left, along with everyone else. And me, I had to show up at home with a bloody nose and no bike. I knew there was no way of hiding this.

DEAD MAN WALKING

I make the walk home and feel like a prisoner who makes his long walk down Death Row on one of those police shows on television. I imagine Mami leaning over me, pointing her finger at me and saying: "I told you so!" At this point, I would have preferred another bloody nose.

As I walk through the front gate to my building, I hear Papo say: "Taco, what the hell happened to you? Who did this to you?", and he turns me around.

"I fell off my bike. That's all.", I said.

"And where did you get that black eye?", Papo continued.

And with that, the beans spill again; but this time without me saying a word.

"Well?", Papo demanded.

"Well what?", I said.

"Tell me who did this to you right now Taco and I'm not fooling around.", Papo said as he looks me in the eyes.

This time I spilled the beans. I even included the advice I got from Don Reyes.

"Taco, you have to go back and get your bike no matter what. If you don't stand up to Hector now, he will keep bullying you. And so will other kids; kids who wouldn't normally be bullies. But now they know you won't do anything, so you would become a target. You have no choice.", Papo said.

"But Don Reyes said I have a choice; and that was not to fight. Maybe Don Reyes is scared?", I answered.

"Taco, Don Reyes is not scared. It's that he fought so much that he didn't want to fight anymore." Papo continued, "You never start a fight. But once it starts, you finish it. Win or lose, you win."

"How so Papo? I understand how you can win and win, but how do you lose and win?", I ask.

Papo said: "Because it's all about standing up. The truth is a bully is just as scared as you are, but the bully picks on smaller kids or kids who are scared. He's hoping you don't stand up to him. So when you fight and lose, the bully knows that you are not an easy target, and you win. And next time he'll think twice about messing with you. And so will everyone else."

And just as he finished, Mami walked up and I thought how much worse could the day get?

"Taco, oh my God! What happened to you!", Mami exclaimed.

"I'm okay Mami. I..."

And before I could finish my sentence, Papo blurted out: "He fell off his bike and it rolled into the street. A truck came along and ran over it. I threw the bike in the dumpster. It was a mess.", Papo said.

"Oh my baby. Thank God you're alright!" Mami said as she grabbed me and hugged me.

Then Papo threw in, "He's lucky to be alive!"

And with those few words, Papo turned my whole day around.

ON THE
RADIO

One day we're on the stoop and Papo is watching over the block, only he's listening to the radio and asking us to quiet down. And then the man on the radio asks a question and Papo runs up the stairs as fast as he can.

And maybe within a minute or two, we hear Papo on the radio. And Papo is talking and we all stop what we're doing and listen to the radio.

Inez yells out to everyone: "Papo's on the radio. Papo's on the radio!"

And everyone gathers around to hear what Papo has to say.

"Who discovered Puerto Rico?", the radio man asks.

"Christopher Columbus, also known as Cristobal Colon, in 1493. He did it on his second voyage.", Papo answers.

"You're right. Congratulations, you're the winner! You'll be our guest on the Radio Rico NY Puerto Rican Day Parade float.", the man says and we all scream and clap.

I'm thinking, how could Columbus discover a place with the Taíno Indians on it? I guess that information only comes when you're Royalty.

And then Papo comes down the stairs, and everyone is clapping and telling Papo how smart he is and asking him how he knew. And when Papo gets to me, he leans over and whispers to me. He says that he's taking Mami and Inez and José and me to the parade, to be proud of Puerto Rico and the people who came here to stay.

PUERTO RICAN PRIDE

Mami woke us up early to get dressed so we could go to the parade.

"Get dressed like you're going to church.", Mami said.

"Are we Mami? Going to church?", José asked.

"No silly, we're going to the parade.", Inez answered.

"But what about church Mami? Won't God get mad?", José asked.

"God won't be mad. He knows where we're going and He'll be there too.", Mami answered.

José looked puzzled.

"Just say a few extra prayers tonight and God will forgive you. He always does; but only if you ask Him to forgive you with all your heart. And you mean it.", Mami said.

So Mami and Inez and José and me went with Papo to the Puerto Rican Day Parade. And the trains in the subway were full of people like us, who were carrying the Puerto Rican flag and standing taller; feeling that it was a good day to be from Puerto Rico. Some people were calling themselves Puerto Ricans and some said they were New York Ricans, although they spelled it differently. And some said they were Boricuas. I think Boricuas were reserved for the Dons and the Doñas.

When we left the subway, Papo took us to a block that had wooden signs that said: "Police Line: Do Not Cross"; so Papo had to show the tickets to the police, before we were allowed to go in. It felt good to go somewhere where you had to be chosen to get in.

We walked to the float and climbed on it and you could feel the excitement in the air; the feeling that something really good was about to happen. And then it did. The float began to move and when it reached the corner, it turned to the left and I could see an ocean of Puerto Rican flags and the ocean of people waving them. They were cheering and clapping, and I could feel butterflies in my stomach; the kind of butterflies that you get when you start a new school and you don't know anyone. And you have to stand up in front of the classroom and tell everyone about yourself.

I looked over at Mami and José and Inez and Papo too; and they looked like I did. And they were smiling and waving back. And it wasn't a normal smile; it was a Christmas Smile.

And the people on the float were dancing and singing: 'Que bonita bandera!' 'What a beautiful flag' was all they kept singing.

I looked at all the flags and realized that the Puerto Rican flag was a sign of something big; of the hopes and dreams of the Puerto Rican people. And the desire to explore; to come to America for a better life. To be bigger than Puerto Rico, you had to leave, but not leave.

And as I stood on that float, on a big street in the middle of the city of New York, I was really proud. I was really proud to have been born on a small island in the Caribbean called... *Puerto Rico.*

NOT ON

WYCKOFF STREET

One day a bad man comes to our block, only we don't know he's bad. I think it was because he was being nice with all the kids, and passing out candy. He said he moved into the same building that Magda lived in and tells us that his name is Carlos.

"Try this kids and if you like it, I'll sell you some more.", Carlos says.

But I have a bad feeling about Carlos. Not the feeling I get where I see things happen before they happen, but the like-you're-about-to-get-in-trouble feeling. Mami used to use the term, "No me cae bien", which meant the person didn't feel right.

Since he makes me feel bad, I stay away from Carlos, but some kids don't and they try the candy. Percy tries too much of it and they rush him to the hospital.

I hear a lot of whispers, and the Dons and the Doñas meet up at the corner bodega to ask why the candy made Percy sick. They should have asked Ibby because Ibby knows about candy; but maybe they were worried that Ibby would try gypping them.

Percy's mother and father are there crying. And the Dons and the Doñas say this can't happen here. Not on Wyckoff Street. So they storm out of the bodega and as they do, the crowd gets bigger. And they chant and scream and continue on to Magda's building, and surround it. Some of them go in and pull Carlos out of the building in his pajamas. As Wyckoff Street is teaching Carlos a lesson, the police show up; a lot of them.

And the police pull Wyckoff Street away from Carlos, and put Carlos in a police car. There are so many people that the police surround the car because they can't move the car; not until more police come. I hear some Police Officers say Carlos should get what he deserves, but this is the law and you can't do that. The crowd is mad, yelling things at Carlos, and Carlos sits in the back of the police car scared and bloodied and beat up.

Finally, there are enough police that they can get Carlos off of Wyckoff Street and the police take him away. But the Dons and Doñas aren't finished. They go back into the Carlos' apartment and empty all of his stuff out onto the street; even his bed. And the next day, the garbage truck comes and takes Carlos' furniture away.

After that, everyone knew that bad men were not welcomed on Wyckoff Street; especially bad men who sold bad candy that made kids sick. Not here; not on Wyckoff Street. And not as long as the Dons and the Doñas kept watch.

PAPO'S ON THE ROOF
WITH A GUN

One night after all of us were already sound asleep, Inez wakes me up and tells me: "Papo's on the roof with a gun. Papo's on the roof with a gun!" My eyes open wide. How could this be? The fun loving Papo who always watched out for us?

Me, I know Papo needs help so I jump out of bed and rush to the window. And in the dead of night, I see fire engines and police cars; and nosey neighbors hoping to see the police make a fool of Papo.

Anyway, I hear screaming and yelling and as I run to the open door, I see Mami standing there blocking the doorway. But I squeeze my way through and see the police leading Papo away in handcuffs. I rush to help Papo and push the Police Officer, and before the Officer has a chance to do anything, Papo yells out.

"Don't hurt him! Please don't hurt him! Let me tell him something. Please?", Papo says.

I know the Police Officer is annoyed, but he lets Papo talk to me. And Papo, handcuffed with his hands behind his back, kneels down.

"Listen Taco, Papo did some bad things. Whenever you do bad things, you have to pay for them. Everyone does ... eventually. Just take care of yourself and watch out for the smaller kids. Would you do that for me?", Papo says.

"You got it Papo." I say as I give him a big hug. A tear streams down my eye and Papo says: "I'll be back." And with that the Police Officer stands Papo up and takes him away. And even though he's going to jail, Papo manages to throw me a smile.

CLOSE CALL

One day I'm sitting on the stoop watching over the kids, like Papo used to, and suddenly it hits me. I feel like my forehead is on fire and I close my eyes. And even though my eyes are closed, I can still see the street, clear as day, and the kids playing on it. I hear police sirens and the sounds of cars speeding and screeching.

And as I look down the block to my left, I see several police cars chasing another car. I watch as that car speeds along and slams into where the kids are playing in the street. And all I can remember is all of the blood all over the cars.

My body leans forward and my eyes open wide. And although I don't know what's happening, I rush down the stairs.

"Quick! Get out of the street, now! Hurry!", I yell.

Almost all together they yell back: "What's wrong Taco?", but they don't move.

"Get the hell on the stoop right now!", I yell so loud that everyone rushes up the stairs.

As I close the gate behind me, I hear police sirens and the sound of cars speeding and screeching. "Quick, into the house!", I tell everyone as we all rush up the stairs and into the hall.

The car slams into several cars where all the kids were just playing. And for maybe a minute or two, everyone is staring at me in shock.

Finally Inez says: "How did you do that?"

"Do what?", I say.

"Yeah, how did you know?", asks Emilio.

"That was a cool magic trick." José continues, "If you show me how you did it, I won't tell Mami you said a bad word."

As I stand there trembling I say: "I was wondering the same thing myself."

SEEING BETTER THINGS

So a few days after predicting the car crash, Mami takes me back to see El Tio again. Blanca told Mami that I had a "regalo"; that I was "gifted" and had special powers. After all, I saw things in my mind before they happened. I didn't think I had special powers like Superman. I think they were trying to get money from Mami, like they did with everyone else; but I went.

I think Mami was hoping that Blanca was right and that I could see money, and maybe the house that Mami always wanted us to have. And I was hoping too. Hoping that even though no one was bigger than God and His Son Jesus, that maybe there were people that could talk to the Saints so that God could get the message.

Mami always said that she thought that we were bigger than Wyckoff Street; that she wanted her kids to be something; José and Inez and me. But that God gave me something extra special to help me along.

I thought back to what Papi had said, and I was hoping that El Tio could show me how to see the winning numbers on the lottery balls, before they came down that long tube.

Then I would buy Mami that big house she wanted, and a car to drive around in. And we wouldn't have to walk or ride in subways or buses. I would make sure that Mami wouldn't have to work until her feet hurt or get up before the sun came up. Or work more than one job.

PAPO IS BACK

José and me are playing stoop ball while Inez is off to the side jumping rope. I bounce the ball too hard off the stairs, and it goes over José's head and bounces across the street. A man in an Army uniform picks it up as I yell across the street: "Excuse me mister. Can you throw the ball back to me?"

The man lifts his head and at first I don't recognize him; he's different. But his smile, it's his smile that I can't forget. It's the same smile I remember as they led him away six months ago in handcuffs.

We run to each other and I jump into his arms. "Papo, you're back?", I say.

"Wow, I should go away everyday. How ya doing champ?", he says as he puts me down.

"I didn't recognize you with the Army uniform and no afro. Are you back for good?", I ask.

"Just came back today to say goodbye. They're shipping me out to Vietnam tomorrow.", he says.

"But Papo, how did you get out of those handcuffs? Is this a disguise?", I ask.

"No Taco." he explains, "The Police gave me a choice: Either go to jail or go into the Army. I don't think I would have liked jail. I figured it was safer in the Army.", Papo says.

"Well, we're glad you're back, even for today.", I say as I give Papo one more hug. "Be careful Papo, and please come back safe. I need help watching these kids. They don't listen.", I tell him.

Papo laughs and says: "You'll do alright kid. You'll do just fine."

And with that, Papo runs up the front stoop and disappears into the building on his way to say goodbye to Don Paco.

In my heart I had hoped that God would watch over Papo, just like Papo watched over us. And I wished that Papo would come back safe; and maybe he would have medals and stories to tell us, just like Don Julio and Don Reyes did.

BOTTLE PATROL

Me and José decided to give Mami some help. After all, we were the men of the family ever since Papi took off.

"How much do you think we could get?", José said as he tied his sneakers.

"I can't wait to see the look on Mami's face. I hope she's proud of us.", I said.

"I bet we can make a million dollars. Maybe a gazillion?", José said with excitement.

"I don't think we can make that much, but every little bit helps.", I said.

We ran down the front stairs and José climbed into our red wagon. I pulled José through the streets of Brooklyn and he was excited as he sat in the wagon.

"This is fun Taco. Go faster. Faster!", José said.

"Okay, but only for a few minutes. We have to start making money.", I said.

The rest of the day we spent collecting as many bottles as we could. We must have looked through every abandoned lot, every subway station, every back alley - for bottles. As the wagon filled up, José had to get out and walk.

"I think we're done", I told José but he wanted to continue.

"C'mon Taco. We can find more.", José said.

"But the wagon is packed. If we fill it too much, the wagon can tip over and the bottles will break. And then we have nothing.", I explained.

"I guess you're right.", José said.

And as the sun began to make it's way across the sky, we started to make our way towards Tito's Bodega. Our hard work was about to pay off.

PICKING UP THE PIECES

We turned the corner, and as we did, me and José ran into Hector and his crew.

"Where are you goin' witcha bottles?", Hector said as the rest of his gang surrounded us.

"These bottles belong to us!", José yelled.

Hector turned to José and said: "Shut up little man before ya get hurt."

As José stepped forward, Enrique stuck his foot out and José tripped and fell forward. Enrique ran over to the wagon and kicked it over. And in an instant, our hopes were smashed to pieces.

I went over to José to check on him. I was mad and didn't know what to do, but then I saw a brick. I picked up the brick and as hard as I could, threw it at Hector's foot. And as Hector leaned forward, I remembered what Papo had said, "Hit the ringleader and the rest will take off."

I closed my eyes and, as hard as I could, I punched Hector in the nose as he bent forward. Hector fell back, grabbed his nose and it began to bleed. And with that, Hector's mighty gang took off, just like Papo had said.

José began to cry and as he wiped his tears he said: "Taco, what do we do now?"

"There's nothing we can do but cash in what we have left", I said.

José climbed into the wagon and we put in the bottles that were left, the ones that didn't break, and we went to Tito's Bodega. We ended up getting only thirty-five cents, but I don't think Hector or his boys would bother us anymore.

PRAY FOR PAPO

One day Don Paco gets a letter from the Army that says that Papo was hurt in that 'Nam place, and that they're sending Papo home. I thought all along with all my prayers to God, that Papo would be alright. I prayed every night for him. I also thought that Papo would come back, just like Don Julio did and maybe bring us Spanish bread once in a while. The sound of Don Papo had a catchy ring to it.

Maybe Papo got hurt because Don Paco used to go to church every Sunday and Papo didn't. Maybe, just maybe, God had forgotten Papo because of that. So when I prayed for Papo, maybe God didn't know who I was talking about.

I knew something wasn't right because there were a lot of whispers when us kids were around, and sometimes the adults would hold their mouths open. Don Paco cried a lot.

And right before Papo came home, Don Paco moved into the apartment under the stairs below us.

I kept wondering if I could get used to this. Having Papo living over us as we slept made me feel safe, since he was always watching over us from the stoop in front of our building.

And then it happened one day. Me and Mami and Inez and José were walking home from school, and we see a "Welcome Home Papo" sign on the front of the building. So I run the rest of the way and knock on Don Paco's' new door below the stairs. The door opens up and I run inside. There, sitting at the table in a metal chair, is Papo.

I drop my book bag and run around the table, and see that the funny metal chair has wheels. Papo wheels himself back from under the table and I stop. Papo, dressed in an Army uniform, has only one leg. Even though he noticed I had stopped, he holds out his arms and I run to him and give him a great big hug.

"Papo, I missed you.", I say.

"Taco, I missed you too. I told you I'd be back. So, Don Paco told me you prayed for me?", he replies.

"Every single day.", I proudly say. "I don't know how you did it?", I ask.

"Did what?", he asks.

"How you used to watch us so well. I can't do it. It's hard enough watching Inez and José.", I continue as he laughs and hugs me again. "So what happened? Are you okay Papo?", I ask.

"Taco, I'm okay. I lost my leg in Vietnam. I stepped on a land mine. It was a big mistake, but it taught me to watch where I was going.", he continues, "At least I get this cool chair. Now we can race down the block."

Papo rolls his chair outside where we meet up with Mami and Inez and José. And as I watch Papo talk, I know he's not the same. Sure he's laughing and telling stories, but he's not the same Papo that left that day.

I wondered if all the young men like Papo, who went to that 'Nam place, came back different. Did they joke around in the day, and cry and have bad dreams at night? Did they fight more with their fathers and have really bad headaches? And did they act the same when they heard a car backfire by saying: "Get Down! Get Down! Charlie's in the light. Ambush! Ambush! Get down!". I kept wondering who Charlie was and why he made Papo so mad at the world and at himself.

THE PAPER
BOY

It didn't start off right away, but I could feel things were going to change. Mami loved life as much as Doňa Maria, but Mami was more practical. She always believed there was a time to laugh and be happy, and there was a time to be serious. Life was a serious business as far as Mami was concerned. She would always say that "you never get out of life alive."

But Doňa Maria always believed that you had to put on a bib, and eat life with a knife and fork; and sometimes with a spoon. I missed Abuela, I mean Doňa Maria, so much. But even though I knew that our loss was God's gain, I was starting to get annoyed with Him. God was taking some of the best people in my life, but I forgave Him. After all, He sent His Son down to save all of us; it was the least I could do.

Things were getting tougher for us. What with Doňa Maria gone, Mami was having trouble picking us up at school and finding work. Mami didn't say it, but I would see her crying as I peeked through the half-open door to the bedroom Mami and Inez shared.

One night, it was time for dinner, but Mami said she wasn't hungry and went to her room. Mami had made rice and she added packets of catsup that she got from the fast food place a few blocks away. I started to eat but I knew Mami needed to eat more than I did, so I acted like I was eating. And when Mami wasn't looking, I put all the rice back in the pot and went to my room.

I knew Mami would find out because my stomach was making noise, so I took some paper out of my notebook and ate that. I ate the paper slowly and I ate until my stomach no longer made any noise. Later, Mami came to me and asked me if I had finished eating and I told her yes.

"Are you sure Taco?" Did you eat because there is still food in the pot?, Mami asked.

"Yes Mami, I did eat.", I said.

Mami listened to my stomach and since it wasn't making any noise, she believed me. So Mami went into the kitchen and ate, but I know Mami. She kept thinking about it, so she came back. But this time Mami wanted answers; especially since Inez and José spilled the beans about me putting back the food.

"Juan Mateo Ortega, tell me the truth.", Mami insisted.

I knew Mami meant business because she called me by three names, just like they do on the news when someone does something really, really bad.

"What did you eat because I know you didn't eat any rice? And your stomach doesn't sound like it's grumbling. So please tell me Juan Mateo Ortega. Tell me.", Mami said as she stared at me.

I knew I couldn't lie to Mami so I told her the truth.

"Mami, I'm sorry. I know you needed the food more than I did, so I ate paper. I'm just a kid, but you need your strength for work.", I answered.

Mami's eyes began to water and she grabbed me and held me tight.

"Thank you Taco for thinking of me. You know I love you lots.", Mami said.

Mami wiped away my tears and I wiped away hers. And I knew that I wasn't in trouble anymore because Mami called me Taco. I also knew that we would be alright because I saw the look in Mami's eyes. It was a look that Mami was going to change our luck no matter what she had to do.

DOŇA MARIA
RETURNS

One night I have this dream that Doňa Maria appears to me. She tells me that she's happy where she is, but she misses us; so every once in a while, Doňa Maria plans to visit me in my dreams. Anyway, she is quite lovely in her silky red dress and black shoes. Doňa Maria always loved her shoes. She then tells me that I will be lucky in the next few days. Then she tells me that there's a Dance Contest on Cloud Nine and off she Tangoes.

I wake up crying, not because I was scared, but because I realized how much I missed my abuela, Doňa Maria, and wished she were still here. I tell Mami about the dream and her eyes fill with tears.

"Mami, should I stop?", I say.

"No Taco, it's that I miss her too.", Mami says. "Just keep on telling your story and don't mind me."

"Okay Mami.", I say and I continue with the story about the red dress, the black shoes and Cloud Nine. I wipe Mami's tears away and she smiles.

"Thank you Taco. That was a sign.", Mami says.

"A sign of what?", I ask.

"Your abuela, Doña Maria, is trying to help us. That's why she left the dance floor. And that shows me how much she loves us.", Mami explains.

"How Mami?", I ask.

Mami continues, "Because nothing could get Doña Maria off the dance floor. Nothing!"

So we all go out. Mami and Inez and José and me. And now everywhere we go, Mami keeps trying to find clues.

On the unemployment line, but Mami doesn't find work. At the Welfare Office, where Mami applies for money and Food Stamps. Waiting on line for Food Stamps. On the subway.

Finally, we get to the Supermarket and Mami pulls out the Food Stamps. And as she shops, she cries.

"Mami, why are you crying?", I say.

"Because I'm in the Supermarket with my kids buying groceries with Food Stamps, that's why! What kind of example is this for my kids?", she answers.

"But Mami, it's not your fault. We only have each other. I wish I was old enough to work.", I say.

Mami looks at me and says: "Never! You're going to school to become someone. All of you are. I will move heaven and earth to do so."

I know Mami would actually move heaven and earth, although when she moves heaven, she may disrupt Doña Maria's dance contest.

TAKING CHANCES

So we're in the supermarket and as we check out, there is a large cut out of a woman in a red dress standing next to a brand new 1972 Red Convertible. The sign says: "Tango Your Way Into A Convertible Sweepstakes".

As we pass the sign, I say: "Mami, that's it. That's it. That's the sign."

With barely a few dollars in her pocket Mami hesitates, I think, because she's practical.

"Mami, but you wanted a sign and here it is.", I tell her.

"Yeah, but Taco this is the only money we have. I can't be dreaming because life is not about taking chances or dreaming. Life is about struggling, broken dreams and empty promises.", Mami answers.

I take out the thirty-five cents that I made from collecting bottles with José and say: "Will this help Mami?".

Mami's eyes fill with tears as she takes the change and goes back to the counter. When Mami returns, she hands a ticket to each one of us: Inez and José and me.

"All of you bring me luck, and I will be nothing without you guys.", Mami says.

Mami kneels down and we rush in for a group hug; just like the ones we used to have with Doňa Maria.

LUCKY US

The phone rings and I pick it up. "Hello, may I speak with Ms. Ortega?", the voice says.

"Hold on please.", I say and cover the phone. "Mami, it's for you.", I say as Mami walks over to the phone, picks it up and begins to listen. And as she does, she begins to smile.

"You're kidding?", she continues "Uh, huh. I can't believe it. Really?".

Mami hangs up the phone.

"Inez, José. Come quickly!", Mami practically screams.

As Inez and José rush in, I hope that it's good news. I think it is because Mami doesn't have that worried look or those watery red eyes.

"Kids, I have great news.", she pauses. "We won the car! We won the car! Taco, you did it!", she yells out as we all hug and kiss and dance around the room.

"Mami, Doňa Maria did it.", I say as Mami begins to tear.

"Taco, you're right.", Mami says as she looks to the sky and makes the Sign of the Cross and mouths: "Thank you Doňa Maria."

Mami takes us out for ice cream to celebrate. And as we sit there enjoying our ice cream together, as a happy family, I can't help but feel that our luck is changing. It's moments like these that make me think how lucky I am to have Mami and Inez and José and memories of Doňa Maria.

And even though she was gone, in my heart, Doňa Maria was sitting at the table eating an ice cream sundae, with plenty of hot fudge, nuts, a mountain of whipped cream, and a big cherry on top. And all dressed up in that red dress and those black shoes.

BEING A FAMILY

Mami woke up early like she did when she was going to work; only she didn't go to work. Instead she woke us up before the sun came up and said: "Today we're having fun. We need to have fun."

After Mami picked up the car that we won, she took us to Manhattan Beach, which is in Brooklyn. That's another one of those riddles that don't seem to make sense. And we all spend the day at the beach being a family. And Papo shows up with Don Paco. And Don Paco starts selling Piraguas right there by our picnic table.

And Mami is barbequing on the grill that has the legs shaped like an 'X'. It's like the 'X' on the treasure maps that show you where the gold is; only now it maps to the spot where you find the good food, the fun and the laughter.

We spend all day together having fun and acting like a real family. And when the sun finally went down on that hot summer day, I couldn't help wishing that it could stay this way.

Mami and Inez and José and me.

And Papo and Don Paco with his Piraguas cart.

Mami was having fun and smiling. Maybe Mami was starting to realize that Papi wasn't coming back. Or maybe, just maybe, Mami realized that Papo changed in 'Nam and that he finally did grow up.

SACRIFICE

So José and me are playing stoop ball and Inez is jumping rope and singing:

> "Engine, engine, number nine.
> Goin down to Caro-li-na.
> If the train falls off the track.
> Do you want your money back?"

And a man walks up and gets in the way of my next play.

"Hello young man. I'm looking for the 'Car for Sale'."

"I'm sorry sir, I don't know of any..." and as I say that, Mami, who is watching from the window, comes down the front stoop and greets the man. Mami and the man go upstairs to talk.

"What happened Taco?", José asks.

"I think Mami is selling the car. The car that abuela, I mean Doña Maria, helped us to win.", I say.

"Can she do that?", José asks.

"Mami can do whatever she wants; she's Mami.", I say.

"I'm sure she has a good reason.", Inez says.

That night at dinner, Mami tells us: "Kids, I sold the car."

"But why Mami?", José asks.

Inez listens, but I question: "Mami, how could you sell it? We wouldn't have to take the bus or the train anymore. And we could go to the beach. And you wouldn't have to wake up early or soak your feet at night."

But Mami has made her decision already; I can see it in her eyes.

"Taco, we need the money more than the car." Mami continues: "And I don't like being on welfare. Sometimes you have to give up something you like or want, for your family. That's what being a parent is all about."

I didn't understand why Mami would sell the car, but I guess you have to be a grown-up, have kids and have that wisdom stuff going to understand.

DREAMING

So Papo's on the roof, but this time with a hammer. And I'm helping him build a ramp so he could roll his wheelchair into the pigeon coop. The pigeon coop was broken; wood, wires, and feathers were stuck here and there. The pigeons had left long ago; probably when Papo went into the Army.

"I can fix it.", Papo said as he wheeled himself closer to the pigeon coop. "Although I'm going to need your help, Taco.", Papo said as he smiled.

And all day long we're up there, Papo and me, on the roof; working on the ramp and the pigeon coop. And Papo's passing on some wisdom about life and the world.

"Taco, you have to have goals in life.", Papo says.

"What's a goal?", I ask.

"Well," Papo continues, "you have dreams; things you want to do in life. Don't you?"

"Yes.", I answer.

"Well, that's good. A goal is a dream with a deadline.", Papo says.

Papo smiled at me, "There's nothing wrong with dreaming; but don't spend too much of your life dreaming. You have to do. **Dream but Do**! Life's too short to dream and not do. The cemetery is full of dreamers who didn't do." Papo continued, "Not sure if you understand, but remember what I just said. One day, it'll come in handy."

And I feel special; that out of all the kids in the neighborhood, I'm the one helping Papo. And I think to myself that this is what it's like to have a father. I always wondered why some fathers couldn't stay, and pass on their wisdom to their kids.

Maybe the world was changing or maybe it was getting harder to work all day and come home at night; and take care of a family. Maybe it was more fun to buzz around like a bee. With all this free love, who wants to be stuck with a family when you could move from flower to flower? And not have some silly kid wanting to be with you all the time, or loving you no matter what you did.

I gave Papo a hug and I squeezed tightly. I did it for many reasons, I guess. I did it because Papo was my best friend, he watched out for us, and was a good listener. I also did it because I loved him; I knew he loved me back because he left and came back, just like he said he would.

And because Papo cared enough to give me something that I could use one day and help make me a Don; *wisdom*.

THIS LITTLE LIGHT

I learned in Miss McAfee's class that the light from the stars and the sun are from the past. Whenever we see their light, since it takes time to get to Earth, we are actually looking into the past. So if the sun ever stopped shining, we wouldn't know for several minutes.

The same thing happens with the people we meet. Some people we meet, and in a few minutes we forget them. But like those far away stars that take years before we find out that they have burned out, there are some people that continue to shine.

Even though Doña Maria was gone, her light had gone out, she continued to shine in my heart. So at times it felt like she never left us. And as time passed, it seemed to take away the sadness and it left me with happy memories.

That's why I stayed away from the park after Doña Maria died. Every time that I saw that tree that she had climbed, I cried. But after a while, when I finally went back to that same park, seeing that tree made me smile, even laugh.

Sure I missed Doña Maria and her "special meals", but now I wasn't hurt. I was happy that out of the entire universe, God had chosen to shine Doña Maria's light on me. And He did it long enough so that when her light finally did stop shining, I could still see it.

PIECES OF PAPO

Then I heard the Police Officer tell Mami that Papo was saying that he was going to jump. It couldn't be. I bolted up the stairs to the roof to help Papo out, to make sure that he would be around for me and to give me advice and hugs; and also to keep me on the right path.

And as I reached the roof door and turned the handle, I could hear the Police Officers saying stuff to Papo and Papo yelling back. About how he could never fit into this world and how no one wanted him. About how he did bad things in 'Nam and here. And how God could never forgive him.

Papo had pushed the ramp we made for the pigeon coop up to the edge of the roof, and rolled his wheelchair up onto it. And there he was.

"I want you, and I love you!", I shouted as I ran onto the roof and towards Papo's wheelchair that was balanced on the edge. And I ran fast. I ran for me and José and Inez and Mami. I ran for all the good times we had. I ran for us to be a family. I knew I could convince Mami she was wrong about Papo. And I knew I could convince Papo that he was wrong about himself. And let Papo know that God would forgive him if he asked for forgiveness with all his heart. And he meant it.

And as I was about to reach Papo, he pushed himself over the edge and fell down into the courtyard, smashing Don Paco's piraguas cart to pieces.

I leaned over the edge and looked at the pieces of Papo. The broken piraguas cart had released white dust into the air. And on that hot summer day, in the middle of July, it began to snow.

MI
FAMILIA

Sometimes people don't realize that 'Familia', or 'Family', are not only those people who are related to you, but those who care about you. The people who take time out to love you, and watch out for you, and give you advice. The people who spy on you and tell you when you're doing wrong; and to go home when it's getting late.

Sometimes other people take better care of you than people in your own family. And sometimes the love we get from our family gives us the strength to go through life no matter what may get in our way. Or to not listen to the people who tell us we can't do this and we can't do that.

Wyckoff Street gave me the rich colors that painted my world. That white building was the canvas. The people were the painting. All the characters, great and small; all of them.

The people who raised and cared for me and taught me what was right and what wasn't. Those who taught me to respect and to be respectful. Those who taught me to love.

And those who made me laugh and taught me that it was okay to laugh at myself. Those colorful people down there on Wyckoff Street were ... *MI FAMILIA*.

TO BE BIGGER
THAN WYCKOFF

Wyckoff Street changed a lot, from the first day I saw that white building until the last day that we pulled away from the curb; in that rented moving truck that Mami drove. Mami and Inez and José and me; sitting next to each other in the front seat, wondering about our future and where we were going.

That 'Nam place had changed people, and people were walking around with signs. And people were marching and yelling and sitting together in circles. And God was calling back a lot of royalty; at least Doña Maria would have company.

Don Paco wasn't the same after Papo did what he did, and neither were me and Mami and Inez and José. Papo tried to make quick money selling powdered candy for bad men like Carlos.

I think Papo was trying to show Mami that he could make money, but Mami said that's not the way to make money; by hurting people. People said Carlos was selling soda, but it didn't look like soda when Papo smashed into the piraguas cart; it looked more like snow.

The trees on Wyckoff Street died with no one to take care of them, and the sidewalks got dirtier. The city came and took out the trees and made the sidewalks bigger.

And Mami. Well, Mami said it was time to go. That the neighborhood was getting too dangerous for a woman alone with three kids; and you couldn't go out at night anymore. And since a lot of the Dons and the Doñas were now with Doña Maria, Mami has fewer spies to watch us.

Don Paco had stopped by earlier in the day to tell Mami that Papo had a Life Insurance policy and that Papo had left him some money, but Don Paco wanted Mami to have it. Don Paco said that Papo had always told him that he loved Mami and Inez and José and me. It felt good to know that I was right all along.

Don Paco also stopped by to give me his special ice shaver machine; the one he used to make piraguas. Now I knew that one day I would own my own Piraguas cart; whether we were here on Wyckoff Street or somewhere else. People always needed a frozen treat to cheer them up; especially under the heat of the summer sun.

And I knew we would be alright. I knew Mami was right; that to be bigger than Wyckoff, we had to leave but not leave. We had to keep Wyckoff within us. We had to keep all the people shining within us, so that they went with us everywhere.

But Mami said that I should write all this down.

"Are you writing in that journal again?", Inez asked.

"Yeah, he puts everything in there, like a book.", José added.

"Why don't you put all this down in your journal, so you could remember; so we all could remember?", Mami said.

I smiled that **Christmas Smile** and said: "I already did Mami. I already did."

GLOSSARY

Abuela – Grandma (in Spanish).

Blanco – the color white (in Spanish).

Bodega – a small grocery store in Hispanic communities, sometimes combined with a wine shop or a liquor store.

Boom Box – slang for radio. A portable stereo system, introduced in the 1970's, that can play radio and recorded music at a high volume. Basically, it's two or more loud speakers, an amplifier, a radio tuner, and a cassette player.

Boricua – (sometimes spelled Boriqua) – term derived from the Taíno word Boriken, in recognition of the island's original Taíno heritage. Boricua is used as a term of endearment and cultural affirmation (see Borinquen).

Borinquen – the original inhabitants of Puerto Rico called the island Borikén or Borinquen, which means: "Great Land of the Valiant and Noble Lord"; the original name for the island of Puerto Rico.

Borinqueneers – nickname for the 65th Infantry Regiment; was an all-volunteer Puerto Rican regiment of the United States Army. Its motto was: "Honor et Fidelitas"; Latin for Honor and Fidelity.

Brownstone – a building constructed of brown Triassic sandstone.

Buccaneer – term that is generally used as a synonym for a pirate. The buccaneers were pirates who attacked Spanish and French shipping in the Caribbean Sea during the late 17th century (the word Taco mistook for Borinqueneers).

Bustelo coffee – also know as Café Bustelo; most recognizable espresso coffee brand in the Hispanic community.

Caribbean – a region consisting of the Caribbean Sea, it's islands and the surrounding coasts.

Coqui – the Puerto Rican tree frog; the common name for several species of small frogs endemic to Puerto Rico.

Dominoes – a game played with domino pieces. A Domino set consists of 28 dominoes of rectangular tiles, with a line dividing its face into two square ends. Each end of the domino is marked with either a number of spots or is blank.

Don – a term of respect. Spanish equivalent of "Sir"; similar to Señor. It was originally a title reserved for royalty, select nobles, and church hierarchs.

Doña – a term of respect. Spanish equivalent of "Madame"; similar to Señora (see Don).

Empanada – a stuffed bread or pastry. Made of flour or cassava flour dough and filled with meat (chicken, ground beef, shrimp, etc.) or cheese with fruit.

En Mi Viejo San Juan – "In My Old San Juan"; one of the most famous Boleros in Puerto Rico; written by Noel Estrada. The song is considered a second national anthem by many Puerto Ricans, especially the Puerto Ricans who live far away from Puerto Rico.

Feliz Navidad – Merry Christmas (in Spanish).

Flan – Spanish egg-custard; a baked custard, similar to crème caramel.

Fulano de Tal – Spanish term for so-and-so, what's-his-name or an unknown person, i.e. Jane or John Doe.

Guayabera – a men's shirt popular in the Caribbean and Latin America. The Guayabera shirt has either two or four patch pockets and two vertical rows of tiny pleats sewn closely together running along the front and back of the shirt, and are made from linen.

Gyp – cheat; fraud; an act of cheating.

Gypper – a person who gyps; a swindler.

Hija – Daughter (in Spanish).

Hijo – Son (in Spanish).

Hispanic – relating to or being a person of Latin American descent, especially Puerto Rican, Cuban, Mexican, South or Central American, or other Spanish culture or origin.

Hombre – Man (in Spanish).

Isla Bonita – Beautiful Island (in Spanish).

La Isla del Encanto – The Island of Enchantment (in Spanish). The island of Puerto Rico is also popularly known as: "La Isla del Encanto".

Latin/Latina/Latino – relating to the people or countries using Romance languages; of or relating to the peoples of countries in the Caribbean or Latin America.

Limber de Leche – a Popsicle made of milk; usually sold in Dixie cups.

Los Tres Reyes Magos – The Three Wise Men (in Spanish). Their feast is celebrated on January 6th; also known as the Feast of the Epiphany. The Three Wise Men went to visit Jesus at His birth, and brought baby Jesus the gifts of Gold, Frankincense and Myrrh.

Mamá – Mom; Mother (in Spanish).

Mami – Mom; Mother (in Spanish).

Mulatto – a person with one white parent and one black parent or a person who has both black ancestry and white ancestry.

Nappy – a term used to refer to the type of hair that grows in a tiny spring-like, corkscrew shape. The overall effect is that despite having relatively fewer actual hairs, it appears (and feels) denser than straight hair; also referred to as 'thick', 'bushy', or 'woolly'.

New York Rican – see Nuyorican.

No Me Cae Bien – Spanish expression that means the person "doesn't feel right" or "the person is not liked."

Nuyorican – term for a New Yorker who is Puerto Rican (or as Taco heard it: New York Rican).

Ortega (Company) – makers of Taco shells as well as various Spanish food products. Where TACO got his nickname.

Papá – Father; Dad (in Spanish).

Papi – Father; Dad (in Spanish).

Pardo – the color Brown (in Spanish).

Pasteles – "Spanish dumplings"; a traditional dish of Puerto Rico and the Spanish-speaking Caribbean; usually served at Christmas and the Three King's Day; sometimes spelled "pastelles".

Piraguas – "PIRamide de AGUA" (Pyramid of Ice). Snow cone.

Piraguero – Piraguas man; one who sells Piraguas.

Primo – Cousin (in Spanish).

Puerto Rico – "Rich Port" (in Spanish); an island in the Caribbean; is composed of an archipelago that includes the main island of Puerto Rico and a number of smaller islands, the largest of which are Vieques, Culebra, and Mona.

Punto y se Acabo – Spanish expression that means: "That's it.", "It's over.", "Finito."

Que Bonita Bandera – What a beautiful flag (in Spanish). The name of a popular song that sings praise to the Puerto Rican flag; a "plena" homage to the Puerto Rican flag; written by Florencio "Flor" Morales Ramos, better known as Ramito.

Regalo – Gift (in Spanish).

Relleno/Relleno de Papa – a dish served consisting of mashed potatoes stuffed with seasoned ground meat and various spices and then deep fried.

Roman Catholic – a Religion; is the world's largest Christian church. About 85% percent of Puerto Ricans.

San Juan – The Capital of Puerto Rico. Originally, the city of San Juan was called Puerto Rico, meaning "rich port", and the entire island was called San Juan. The capital and the island's names were later accidentally switched.

Santería – an Afro-Caribbean belief system brought to Puerto Rico from Cuba.

Santero – the high priest of the religion of Santeria.

Spanish Bread – also known as "Pan Dulce", which is Spanish for "sweet bread"; is primarily eaten at breakfast.

Suegra – Mother-in-law (in Spanish).

Taco – a traditional Mexican dish composed of a corn or wheat tortilla folded or rolled around a filling. A taco can be made with a variety of fillings, including beef, chicken, seafood, vegetables and cheese.

Tarot/Tarot Cards – A special pack of cards used mainly for fortune-telling or for reading a person's future. The Tarot pack has a total of 78 cards consisting of four (4) suits of 14 cards each (the minor arcana), and 22 other cards (the major arcana).

Taíno Indian/Taíno – The original inhabitants of Puerto Rico are the Taíno, meaning "good" or "noble".

Tía – Aunt (in Spanish).

Tío – Uncle (in Spanish).

Uno Más – One More (in Spanish).

Vietnam/Vietnam War – also known as the Vietnam Conflict; was a Cold War military conflict that occurred in Vietnam, Laos, and Cambodia from November 1, 1955 to April 30, 1975 when Saigon fell. Often referred to as 'Nam.

TACO

JD's Quotes:

Remember, you're never too **old** to start something **new**.

John E. DeJesus

The most buried treasures lie in the cemetery. There lies buried the dreams that never came true, the goals that were never reached, the inventions that were never created and the books that were never written.

Don't be a buried treasure.

John E. DeJesus

John E. DeJesus

Author Q & A

Why did you become a writer?

Honestly, there has always been a writer within me. In school, the teachers would ask me to write less because I always wrote a paragraph when a line or two would suffice. So it's been bubbling up inside me. I just decided to let the proverbial "genie" out of the bottle. I started about four years ago writing screenplays. This is my first foray into writing a book. It's been quite a journey.

What inspired you to write the book?

One rule of writing is "write what you know". It's a good rule but it's not totally accurate. You have to use your imagination and make up characters and places and situations. My life is not that exciting. I grew up in Brooklyn on a block similar to the one that Taco grew up on. I took some stories and ideas of things that happened in my life and added a whole lot of imagination.

Are you TACO?

I am not Taco nor was that ever my nickname. But now, it seems that it will eventually become my nickname as everyone keeps calling me Taco. As far as nicknames go, I guess it's as good as any.

TACO

Author Q & A (cont.)

Do or did any of your characters exist?

Yes and no. Yes, there were people like the characters in the book. But the characters in the book are a mix of people so no there are no individual persons that you can say are Dona Maria or Don Paco or Tio Alberto.

Where did you come up with the name Taco?

I recall as a child eating food products made by a company called Ortega; such as Ortega Tacos. I know Ortega is a common Spanish name in Puerto Rico.

Will there be a sequel to Taco?

I have had people ask me to write a book about Taco after he left Wyckoff Street. I am considering that. Actually, Taco was a much bigger book, but I had to cut it down in order to keep the cost of the book reasonable. I thought of possibly releasing the "original" larger book as: "The Big Taco". But when I pitched the idea, everyone thought I was pitching a book about Taco as a teenager; hence, the Big Taco. I am considering doing one or the other. Who knows? Maybe I will end up doing both.

John E. DeJesus

Author Q & A (cont.)

If you had advice for writing, what would that be?

Write! That's my advice. Write and keep writing. The more you write the more experience you will get and the better you will become. Take classes, join groups of fellow writers, read books on writing, read all kinds of books. If you are selecting a specific genre, read books on that genre. Hone your craft. Make up stories. Write what you know. Write what you don't know. Write what you think you know. Write what you think you don't know. Just write. If a title comes to you, write it down. If a name comes to you, write it down. Carry a notebook. Write ideas, thoughts, wishes, desires. Write! I would say that you probably use 3-5% of what you write, if that, for books or screenplays. But I liken writing to Edison's light bulbs. He made tons of them but only a few worked. Write On!

TACO

Poetry

Who Will Mourn My Death
By John E. DeJesus

Who will mourn my death
When all is said and done.
When all the words are spoken
And all the hymns are sung.

When I am covered from head to toe
With earth and dirt and sand.
When I am finally laid to rest
And no longer walk this land.

Who will mourn my death
Will It be only me?
Or just some old friends that I knew
Or just my family?

Or maybe my ashes will just take flight
Like specs upon the wind.
And land into the eye of someone
Who is neither friend nor kin.

John E. DeJesus

Who Will Mourn My Death (cont.)
By John E. DeJesus

And when I finally happen into
The eye of someone other.
Than a friend or someone that I knew
A brother, child, or mother.

Will then that be the only eye,
That sheds a tear for me?
Just tell me who will mourn my death,
And all I came to be?

TACO

John E. DeJesus

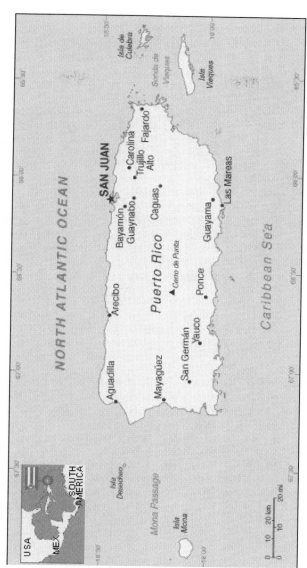

The Island of Puerto Rico

TACO

The Flag of Puerto Rico
"Que Bonita Bandera"

The Puerto Rican flag consists of 5 alternate red and white stripes. On the left of the flag is a single white five-pointed star resting in a blue triangle. The symbolism is explained thus. The white star stands for the Commonwealth of Puerto Rico while the three sides of the equilateral triangle together represent the three branches of the Republican government (executive, legislative and judicial branches). The three red strips symbolize the blood that feeds those parts of the government. The two white stripes symbolizing the rights of man and the freedom of the individual, are a perpetual reminder of the need for vigilance of a democratic government is to be preserved. The flag is only flown in company of the U.S. flag. The Puerto Rican flag was adopted in July 25, 1952.

John E. DeJesus

The Coat of Arms of Puerto Rico

Joannes Est Nomen Ejus, Latin "John is his name". The coat of arms of **Puerto Rico** was first granted by the Spanish Crown in 1511, making it the oldest heraldic achievement still currently in use in the Americas.

Made in the USA
Lexington, KY
27 November 2019

57772275R00107